I'd like to dedicate this book to all the schools I visit – but particularly Hythe Primary School in Southampton, where Miss Brenig-Jones turned my poem 'Let No One Steal Your Dreams' into their school song. (Look up 'Hythe Primary School – Let No One Steal Your Dreams' on YouTube and see the fantastic job they did.)

It's a special poem for me – and where the idea for this book first started.

Special thanks to everyone at Macmillan, especially Gaby Morgan, Fliss Stevens, Tracey Ridgewell, George Lester, Charlotte Copping and Alyx Price.

Contents

Introduction

Hello and welcome to *100 Brilliant Poems for Children*.

There will never be a definitive hundred brilliant poems . . . but I know that these are a hundred brilliant poems.

I wanted to choose poems that have some sort of longevity: poems that are already classics, poems that are modern classics and poems that I feel will have a life beyond this book and become classics in their own right.

The collection starts with my own 'Let No One Steal Your Dreams' – in fact, the idea for the collection started with that poem. It's that feeling we are looking for – poems that inspire, and that are aspirational and entertaining in every way.

I've chosen poems by my favourite poets, poems that I wish I'd written, poems that I'll be forever jealous of and poems that have inspired me.

I also wanted to include a few pieces that haven't been seen before in a book for children. Words that have meant something to me, words that have touched me at particular times. I say words – as some of them began as songs I've played again and again, but with words that I feel work well as stand-alone poems. Not many songwriters are poets, but some are and I've included a few here – Billy Bragg, Michael McDermott, Nigel Stonier, Martin Stephenson, Henry Priestman (The Christians), Miles Hunt (The Wonder Stuff) and Stan Cullimore (The Housemartins). Check them out – I hope you like them. No, I'll rephrase that – I hope you *love* them.

Enjoy!

Paul Cookson

Let No One Steal Your Dreams

Let no one steal your dreams
Let no one tear apart
The burning of ambition
That fires the drive inside your heart

Let no one steal your dreams
Let no one tell you that you can't
Let no one hold you back
Let no one tell you that you won't

Set your sights and keep them fixed
Set your sights on high
Let no one steal your dreams
Your only limit is the sky

Let no one steal your dreams
Follow your heart
Follow your soul
For only when you follow them
Will you feel truly whole

Set your sights and keep them fixed
Set your sights on high
Let no one steal your dreams
Your only limit is the sky

Paul Cookson

My Colours

These are
My colours,
One by one:

Red –
The poppies
Where I run.

Orange –
Summer's
Setting sun.

Yellow –
Farmers'
Fields of corn.

Green –
The clover
On my lawn.

Blue –
The sea
Where fishes spawn.

Violet –
The dancing
Heather.

A rainbow
They make
All together.

Colin West

A Morning Song

For the First Day of Spring

Morning has broken
Like the first morning,
Blackbird has spoken
Like the first bird.
Praise for the singing!
Praise for the morning!
Praise for them, springing
From the first Word.

Sweet the rain's new fall
Sunlit from heaven,
Like the first dewfall
In the first hour.
Praise for the sweetness
Of the wet garden,
Sprung in completeness
From the first shower.

Mine is the sunlight!
Mine is the morning
Born of the one light
Eden saw play.
Praise with elation,
Praise every morning
Spring's re-creation
Of the First Day!

Eleanor Farjeon

Slithering Silver

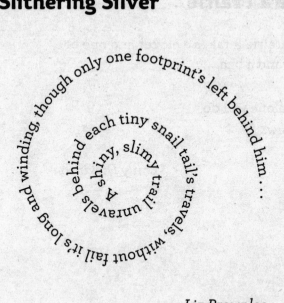

though only one footprint's left behind him …
winding,
long and
it's
tail
behind each tiny snail tail's travels,
without
unravels
A shiny, slimy trail.

Liz Brownlee

To Make a Prairie

To make a prairie it takes a clover and one bee,
One clover, and a bee,
And revery.
The revery alone will do,
If bees are few.

Emily Dickinson

For Every Thing There Is a Season

For every thing there is a season, and a time for every
    purpose under the heaven:
A time to be born, and a time to die;
A time to plant, and a time to pluck up that which is
    planted;
A time to kill, and a time to heal;
A time to break down, and a time to build up;
A time to weep, and a time to laugh;
A time to mourn, and a time to dance;
A time to cast away stones, and a time to gather stones
    together;
A time to embrace, and a time to refrain from
    embracing;
A time to get, and a time to lose;
A time to keep, and a time to cast away;
A time to rend, and a time to sew;
A time to keep silence, and a time to speak;
A time to love, and a time to hate;
A time of war, and a time of peace.

From *Ecclesiastes*

Conquer

Five children clasping mittens
could not hug the entire trunk.
Whole hands could hide in the folds of its bark.
James, the tallest boy in class,
could sit on a root,
his feet would not touch the ground.

Every classroom faced the playground,
every child could see the tree.
Leaves beckoning.
Conkers swelling.

As the bells rang
we'd march to the tree,
sticks in hand,
eyes fixed on the mace-like horse chestnuts.
Green spikes hungry to prick
our minds obsessed by the jewels within.

Joseph Coelho

There Will Come Soft Rains

There will come soft rains and the smell of
   the ground,
And swallows circling with their shimmering sound;

And frogs in the pools, singing at night,
And wild plum trees in tremulous white,

Robins will wear their feathery fire,
Whistling their whims on a low fence-wire;

And not one will know of the war, not one
Will care at last when it is done.

Not one would mind, neither bird nor tree,
If mankind perished utterly;

And Spring herself, when she woke at dawn,
Would scarcely know that we were gone.

Sara Teasdale

The Apple Raid

Darkness came early, though not yet cold;
Stars were strung on the telegraph wires;
Street lamps spilled pools of liquid gold;
The breeze was spiced with garden fires.

That smell of burnt leaves, the early dark,
Can still excite me but not as it did
So long ago when we met in the Park –
Myself, John Peters and David Kidd.

We moved out of town to the district where
The lucky and wealthy had their homes
With garages, gardens, and apples to spare
Ripely clustered in the trees' green domes.

We chose the place we meant to plunder
And climbed the wall and dropped down to
The secret dark. Apples crunched under
Our feet as we moved through the grass and dew.

The clusters on the lower boughs of the tree
Were easy to reach. We stored the fruit
In pockets and jerseys until all three
Boys were heavy with their tasty loot.

Safe on the other side of the wall
We moved back to town and munched as we went.
Wonder if David remembers at all
That little adventure, the apples' fresh scent?

Strange to think that he's fifty years old,
That tough little boy with scabs on his knees;
Stranger to think that John Peters lies cold
In an orchard in France beneath apple trees.

Vernon Scannell

Stopping by Woods on a Snowy Evening

Whose woods these are I think I know.
His house is in the village though;
He will not see me stopping here
To watch his woods fill up with snow.

My little horse must think it queer
To stop without a farmhouse near
Between the woods and frozen lake
The darkest evening of the year.

He gives his harness bells a shake
To ask if there is some mistake.
The only other sound's the sweep
Of easy wind and downy flake.

The woods are lovely, dark and deep,
But I have promises to keep,
And miles to go before I sleep,
And miles to go before I sleep.

Robert Frost

Den to Let

To let
One self-contained
Detached den.
Accommodation is compact
Measuring one yard square.
Ideal for two eight-year-olds
Plus one small dog
Or two cats
Or six gerbils.
Accommodation consists of:
One living room
Which doubles as kitchen
Bedroom
Entrance-hall
Dining room
Dungeon
Space capsule
Pirate boat
Covered wagon
Racing car
Palace
Aeroplane
Junk-room
And lookout post.
Property is southward facing
And can be found
Within a short walking distance
Of the back door

At bottom of garden.
Easily found in the dark
By following the smell
Of old cabbages and tea bags.
Convenient escape routes
Past rubbish dump
To Seager's Lane
Through hole in hedge,
Or into next door's garden;
But beware of next door's rhinoceros
Who sometimes thinks he's a poodle.
Construction is of
Sound corrugated iron
And roof doubles as shower
During rainy weather.
Being partially underground,
Den makes
A particularly effective hiding place
When in a state of war
With older sisters
Brothers
Angry neighbours
Or when you simply want to be alone.
Some repair work needed
To north wall
Where Mr Spence's foot came through
When planting turnips last Thursday.
With den go all contents
Including:
One carpet – very smelly

One teapot – cracked
One woolly penguin –
No beak and only one wing
One unopened tin
Of sultana pud
One hundred and three *Beanos*
Dated 1983–1985
And four *Rupert* annuals.
Rent is free
The only payment being
That the new occupant
Should care for the den
In the manner to which it has been accustomed
And on long summer evenings
Heroic songs of days gone by
Should be loudly sung
So that old and glorious days
Will never be forgotten.

Gareth Owen

Lone Mission

On evenings, after cocoa
(blackout down and sealed)
I would build plasticine cities
on green lino
and bomb them with encyclopedias
(dropped from ceiling level)
from my Lancaster Bomber
built
(usually)
from table, box and curtains
turret made of chairs
radio and gas masks
tray and kitchen ware.
But:
    Aircrew were my problem
    gunners mid and rear
    radio and bomber
    nav. And engineer.

Each night I flew lone missions
through flack both hot and wild
and learnt it wasn't easy
to be an only child.

Peter Dixon

The River

The River's a wanderer,
A nomad, a tramp,
He doesn't choose one place
To set up his camp.

The River's a winder,
Through valley and hill
He twists and he turns,
He just cannot be still.

The River's a hoarder,
And he buries down deep
Those little treasures
That he wants to keep.

The River's a baby,
He gurgles and hums
And sounds like he's happily
Sucking his thumbs.

The River's a singer,
As he dances along
The countryside echoes
The notes of his song.

The River's a monster,
Hungry and vexed,
He's gobbled up trees
And he'll swallow you next.

Valerie Bloom

Nation's Ode to the Coast

A big fat sky and a thousand shrieks
The tide arrives and the timber creaks
A world away from the working week
Où est la vie nautique?
That's where the sea comes in . . .

Dishevelled shells and shovelled sands,
Architecture all unplanned
A spade 'n' bucket wonderland
A golden space, a Frisbee and
The kids and dogs can run and run
And not run in to anyone
Way out! Real gone!
That's where the sea comes in

Impervious to human speech,
Idle time and tidal reach
Some memories you can't impeach
A nice cuppa splosh and a round of toast
A cursory glance at the morning post
A pointless walk along the coast
That's what floats my boat the most
That's where the sea comes in

Now, voyager – once resigned
Go forth to seek and find
The hazy days you left behind
Right there in the back of your mind
Where lucid dreams begin
With rolling dunes and rattling shale
The shoreline then a swollen sail
Picked out by a shimmering halo
That's where the sea comes in

Could this be luck by chance?
Eternity in a second glance
A universe beyond romance
That's where the sea comes in . . .
Yeah, that's where the sea comes in . . .

John Cooper Clarke

With the Waterfalls

I'm miles away today: I'm with the waterfalls.
I won't be round to play so please don't try to call.

I'm out beyond the boundary in the shimmer-spray.
Thick folds of mist surround me but I know the way.

I've walked towards the roar a thousand times before.
I'm miles away today: I'm with the waterfalls.

Matt Goodfellow

Song of the Iceberg

Once I was a dewdrop
A million years ago
Rose up on a misty day
Into the clouds and rolled away

Reborn as a raindrop
I fell to earth as rain
To rise and fall and rise and fall
And rise and fall again

Rise and fall, freshwater and brine
Rise and fall and rise and fall until the end of time
Rise and fall, freshwater and brine
Rise and fall and rise and fall until the end of time

Once I was a snowflake
Ten thousand years ago
Drifting in a blizzard deep
Fell into a frozen sleep

Reborn as an iceberg
We calved at Baffin Bay
And waited for the moon tides
To carry us away

A single fleeting moment
In a vast ocean of time
Floating on a night so calm
Pass me by, I mean no harm

A mountain made of raindrops
Goes drifting on its way
And dreams of making rainbows
On some distant summer's day

Billy Bragg

No Man Is an Island

No man is an island,
Entire of itself,
Every man is a piece of the continent,
A part of the main.
If a clod be washed away by the sea,
Europe is the less.
As well as if a promontory were.
As well as if a manor of thy friend's
Or of thine own were:
Any man's death diminishes me,
Because I am involved in mankind,
And therefore never send to know for whom the
    bell tolls;
It tolls for thee.

John Donne

Changed

For months he taught us, stiff-faced.
His old tweed jacket closely buttoned up,
his gestures careful and deliberate.

We didn't understand what he was teaching us.
It was as if a veil, a gauzy bandage, got between
what he was showing us and what we thought we saw.

He had the air of a gardener, fussily protective
of young seedlings, but we couldn't tell
if he was hiding something or we simply couldn't see it.

At first we noticed there were often scraps of leaves
on the floor where he had stood. Later, thin wisps
of thread like spider's web fell from his jacket.

Finally we grew to understand the work. And on that day
he opened his jacket, which to our surprise
seemed lined with patterned fabric of many
shimmering hues.

Then he smiled and sighed. And with this movement
the lining rippled and instantly the room was filled
with a flickering storm of swirling butterflies.

Dave Calder

I Hope I Always

I hope I always have your friendship
I hope I always have your trust
While there's a you and there's a me
I hope there'll always be an us
I hope I always keep on listening
I hope I always keep awake
I hope I keep some of those promises
That are easier to break

I hope I always ask the question
I hope I always smell the rose
I hope I choose the bigger picture
Above the king's new clothes
I hope I always know my dark side
And all I need to rise above
I hope I always stay worthy
Of the people that I love

I hope I always know the time to stop
The time to push my luck
The time to stand up and be counted
The time to sit down and shut up
I hope I always find the threads
Then remember how to spin them
I hope I always want the details
Even when the devil's in them

I hope I always count my blessings
I hope I always chase the sun
Sweat and toil when there's a reason
But still remember to have to fun
I hope I see off fear and anger
And step off their slippery slope
I hope I always, always love
I hope I always, always hope

Nigel Stonier

The Night Mail

This is the night mail crossing the border,
Bringing the cheque and the postal order,
Letters for the rich, letters for the poor,
The shop at the corner and the girl next door.
Pulling up Beattock, a steady climb:
The gradient's against her, but she's on time.
Past cotton-grass and moorland boulder,
Shovelling white steam over her shoulder,
Snorting noisily as she passes
Silent miles of wind-bent grasses.
Birds turn their heads as she approaches,
Stare from the bushes at her blank-faced coaches.
Sheepdogs cannot turn her course;
They slumber on with paws across.
In the farm she passes no one wakes,
But a jug in a bedroom gently shakes.

Dawn freshens. Her climb is done.
Down towards Glasgow she descends,
Towards the steam tugs yelping down a glade of
    cranes,
Towards the fields of apparatus, the furnaces
Set on the dark plain like gigantic chessmen.
All Scotland waits for her:
In the dark glens, beside the pale-green lochs,
Men long for news.

Letters of thanks, letters from banks,
Letters of joy from girl and boy,

Receipted bills and invitations
To inspect new stock or visit relations,
And applications for situations,
And timid lovers' declarations,
And gossip, gossip from all the nations,
News circumstantial, news financial.
Letters with holiday snaps to enlarge in,
Letters with faces scrawled in the margin.
Letters from uncles, cousins and aunts,
Letters to Scotland from the South of France,
Letters of condolence to Highlands and Lowlands,
Notes from overseas to the Hebrides;
Written on paper of every hue,
The pink, the violet, the white and the blue,
The chatty, the catty, the boring, the adoring,
The cold and official and the heart's outpouring,
Clever, stupid, short and long,
The typed and the printed and the spelt all wrong.

Thousands are still asleep,
Dreaming of terrifying monsters
Or a friendly tea beside the band in Cranston's or
  Crawford's;
Asleep in working Glasgow, asleep in well-set Edinburgh,
Asleep in granite Aberdeen,
They continue their dreams,
But shall wake soon and hope for letters,
And none will hear the postman's knock
Without a quickening of the heart.
For who can bear to feel himself forgotten?

W. H. Auden

From a Railway Carriage

Faster than fairies, faster than witches,
Bridges and houses, hedges and ditches;
And charging along like troops in a battle,
All through the meadows the horses and cattle:
All of the sights of the hill and the plain
Fly as thick as driving rain;
And ever again in the wink of an eye,
Painted stations whistle by.

Here is a child who clambers and scrambles,
All by himself and gathering brambles;
Here is a tramp who stands and gazes;
And there is the green for stringing the daisies!
Here is a cart run away in the road
Lumping along with man and load;
And here is a mill and there is a river,
Each a glimpse and gone forever!

Robert Louis Stevenson

The Magic of the Mind

I've read in books of magic lands
So very far away,
Where genies pop up out of lamps
And magic creatures play.
Where wizards weave their magic spells
And dragons breathe out fire,
Where just one wish gives young and old
Their every heart's desire.

Those lands, of course, are just in books,
But if you try real hard,
Those magic places come to life
Right in your own back yard.
For sitting quietly in the sun
On a lazy Summer's day
You can sit and smile and dream you're there
In those lands so far away.

And as the sunshine warms your mind
You're in those golden lands,
With wizards, genies, dragons, spells,
And cut-throat pirate bands.
You're saving damsels in distress,
You're fighting deadly duels,
You're banqueting in marbled halls,
You're decked in priceless jewels.

You're there, you're there, no need for books,
So real and oh so clear,
So marvellous and so magical,
To touch and smell and hear.
Just sitting there in golden sun
You leave your cares behind,
And go to magic places
In the Magic of the Mind.

Clive Webster

What Will I Put in My Suitcase When I Go to Visit the Stars?

A feather cushion for a soft landing,
A wetsuit for a streamlined flight,
Fifteen memory cards for a long-lasting camera,
A handkerchief, stitched with my father's initial,
to leave between the spheres.

A cardboard box of secret wishes from my friends,
A map of the constellations,
A magnifying glass to scrutinize the stars,
A telescope to look back down to earth,
A pair of silver-sequinned trousers.

Six bags of Space Dust popping candy,
A tartan blanket in case the night is cold,
Two apples from my garden –
one to give to someone living there,
the other to spill into the heavens
from the greatest height
as I lean in to watch it disappear.

Chrissie Gittins

The Magic of the Brain

Such a sight I saw:
An eight-sided kite surging up into a cloud
Its eight tails streaming out as if they were one.
It lifted my heart as starlight lifts the head
Such a sight I saw.

And such a sound I heard:
One bird through dim winter light as the day was
    closing
Poured out a song suddenly from an empty tree.
It cleared my head as water refreshes the skin
Such a sound I heard.

Such a smell I smelled:
A mixture of roses and coffee, of green leaf and
    warmth.
It took me to gardens and summer and cities abroad,
Memories of meetings as if my past friends were here
Such a smell I smelled.

Such soft fur I felt:
It wrapped me around, soothing my winter-cracked
    skin,
Not gritty or stringy or sweaty but silkily warm
As my animal slept on my lap, and we both breathed
    content
Such soft fur I felt.

Such food I tasted:
Smooth-on-tongue soup, and juicy crackling of meat,
Greens like fresh fields, sweet-on-your-palate peas,
Jellies and puddings and fragrance of fruit they are
    made from
Such good food I tasted.

Such a world comes in:
Far world of the sky to breathe in through your nose
Near world you feel underfoot as you walk on the land.
Through your eyes and your ears and your mouth and
    your brilliant brain
Such a world comes in.

Jenny Joseph

A Feather from an Angel

Anton's box of treasures held
a silver key and a glassy stone,
a figurine made of polished bone
and a feather from an angel.

The figurine was from Borneo,
the stone from France or Italy,
the silver key was a mystery
but the feather came from an angel.

We might have believed him if he'd said
the feather fell from a bleached white crow
but he always replied, 'It's an angel's, I know,
a feather from an angel.'

We might have believed him if he'd said,
'An albatross let the feather fall.'
But he had no doubt, no doubt at all,
his feather came from an angel.

'I thought I'd dreamt him one night,' he'd say,
'but in the morning I knew he'd been there;
he left a feather on my bedside chair,
a feather from an angel.'

And it seems that all my life I've looked
for the sort of belief that nothing could shift,
something simple and precious as Anton's gift,
a feather from an angel.

Brian Moses

Angels

We are made from light.
Called into being we burn
Brighter than the silver white
Of hot magnesium.
More sudden than yellow phosphorus
We are the fire of heaven:
Blue flames and golden ether.

We are from stars.
Spinning beyond the farthest galaxy
In an instant gathered to this point
We shine, speak out messages and go,
Back to the brilliance.
We are not separate, not individual,
We are what we are made of. Only
Shaped sometimes into tall-winged warriors,
Our faces solemn as swords,
Our voices joy.

The skies are cold;
Suns do not warm us;
Fire does not burn itself.
Only once we touched you
And felt a human heat.
Once, in the brightness of the frost.
Above the hills, in glittering starlight,
Once, we sang.

Jan Dean

35

The Dragon Who Ate Our School

The day the dragon came to call,
she ate the gate, the playground wall
and, slate by slate, the roof and all,
the staffroom, gym and entrance hall,
and every classroom, big or small.

So...
She's undeniably great.
She's absolutely cool,
the dragon who ate
the dragon who ate
the dragon who ate our school.

Pupils panicked. Teachers ran.
She flew at them with wide wingspan.
She slew a few and then began
to chew through the lollipop man,
two parked cars and a transit van.

Wow...!
She's undeniably great.
She's absolutely cool,
the dragon who ate
the dragon who ate
the dragon who ate our school.

She bit off the head of the head.
She said she was sad he was dead.
He bled and he bled and he bled.
And as she fed, her chin went red
and then she swallowed the cycle shed.

Oh . . .
She's undeniably great.
She's absolutely cool,
the dragon who ate
the dragon who ate
the dragon who ate our school.

It's thanks to her that we've been freed.
We needn't write. We needn't read.
Me and my mates are all agreed,
we're very pleased with her indeed.
So clear the way, let her proceed.

Cos . . .
She's undeniably great.
She's absolutely cool,
the dragon who ate
the dragon who ate
the dragon who ate our school.

There was some stuff she couldn't eat.
A monster forced to face defeat,
she spat it out along the street –
the dinner ladies' veg and meat
and that pink stuff they serve for sweet.

But ...
She's undeniably great.
She's absolutely cool,
the dragon who ate
the dragon who ate
the dragon who ate our school.

Nick Toczek

Evidence of a Dragon
(notes taken from The Dragon Tracker's Manual*)*

Large enough, most can be
identified from a safe distance.

(However, the Redhill Ridge-back
is only the size of a puppy
and therefore hides with ease.)

When seeking dragons, take care
to look for telltale signs –
trees may be stripped bare
of leaves, bark will be charred.
It should not be hard
to find scorch marks on walls
and, of course, the smouldering
remains of buildings
are a good indicator
that a dragon has passed your way.

After a dragon has called –
houses, shops and town centres
are deserted –
front doors left open,
unfinished meals on tabletops,
and TVs still blaring.

A daring dragon will rob shops,
leaving the butcher's empty.
The chewed remains of cattle are
a dead giveaway.

Dragon tracks are hard to miss –
even by the least experienced of hunters.
So too are places where trees,
bushes and sheds have been blown over.

(Remember – the force from
a full-grown dragon's wings
is as powerful as a hurricane.)

Of course, claw marks raking the earth,
turf scratched and scars on pavements
or tarmac roads all indicate a dragon's presence.

Fragments of broken shell
and piles of jewels
suggest an abandoned dragon's nest
and should be treated with caution
in case the owner returns
and burns anyone
caught loitering nearby.

Any sighting of a dragon flying,
at rest, or on the move
should be reported at once
to the DPD
(Dragon Prevention Department),
who will attempt to tempt
the dragon to kiss a princess
and fall into a hundred years
of blissful sleep.

PS
Vacancies exist
for any princess
who will not be missed!

Pie Corbett

The Long Grass

I lost my favourite football
in the long grass
thirty years ago.
We searched for hours,
for days, for weeks on end.
But could we find it? No.
The air will have escaped by now.

The fountain pen
my brother gave me
disappeared back then,
left for a moment;
but I can't remember
where or when.
Who waved a magic wand?

Somewhere between the front door
and eternity
I lost a bunch of keys.
Climbed on chairs to search for them.
Searched on hands and knees.
I asked my friends.
They have no news.

The wallet
given as a Christmas present?
Gone.
Gone with all its money
and the scraps of paper I had written on.
Will someone ever
hand it in?

I misplace people's names.
Their faces I remember, yes,
but who they are
and when we met
I cannot even guess.
My memory is decomposing
in the grass.

My toys have gone.
The diary I kept
when I was seventeen:
its list of favourite films,
the dreams of who I might have been.
Could they have wound up
in the bin?

With one brief chapter
left to read
I left my book
somewhere sensible.
I've no idea where.
Will you help me look?
I can tell you what each character is like.

I miss my father too.
I'd like to find him
but I don't know how.
Perhaps he's wading
through the long grass even now,
calling our names;
trying to get home.

Stephen Knight

Home

Everywhere we wander
Everywhere our spirits roam
Everywhere we wander
Love will guide us home

Even through the strongest wind
Far from our darkest sin
There's a light within us
They call it home

Home isn't always that house you were born
Just a light where love is strong
Everywhere we wander
Love will guide us home

Martin Stephenson

My Mother Smells . . .

My mother smells of pizza,
toast and shepherd's pie,
my mother smells of ironing
and washing almost dry.

My mother smells of hair gel,
her cut is short and slick,
and sometimes if the baby's ill
my mother smells of sick.

My mother smells of perfume
although she's getting on.
My mother smells of 'girls' night out',
she's almost forty-one!

My mother smells of safety,
is that so of other mums?
My mother smells of worry
when the debit statement comes.

My mother smells of patience,
but if I'm doing wrong
my mother smells of very cross
which doesn't last that long.

My mother smells of many things,
of chips, a duvet cover,
styling mousse, soiled bibs, and love . . .
these smells are all my mother.

Stewart Henderson

Tank Park Salute

Kiss me goodnight and say my prayers
Leave the light on at the top of the stairs
Tell me the names of the stars up in the sky
A tree taps on the windowpane
That feeling smothers me again
Daddy is it true that we all have to die?
At the top of the stairs
Is darkness

I closed my eyes and when I looked
Your name was in the memorial book
And what had become of all the things we'd planned?
I accepted the commiserations
Of all your friends and your relations
But there's some things I still don't understand
You were so tall
How could you fall?

Some photographs of a summer's day
A little boy's lifetime away
Is all I've left of everything we've done
Like a pale moon in a sunny sky
Death gazes down as I pass by
To remind me that I'm but my father's son
I offer up to you
This tribute
I offer up to you
This tank park salute

Billy Bragg

Daddy Fell into the Pond

Everyone grumbled. The sky was grey.
We had nothing to do and nothing to say.
We were nearing the end of a dismal day,
And there seemed to be nothing beyond,
THEN
Daddy fell into the pond!

And everyone's face grew merry and bright,
And Timothy danced for sheer delight.
'Give me the camera, quick, oh quick!
He's crawling out of the duckweed.' *Click!*

Then the gardener suddenly slapped his knee,
And doubled up, shaking silently,
And the ducks all quacked as if they were daft
And it sounded as if the old drake laughed.

Oh, there wasn't a thing that didn't respond
WHEN
Daddy fell into the pond!

Alfred Noyes

Gran Can You Rap?

Gran was in her chair she was taking a nap
When I tapped her on the shoulder to see if she could
    rap.
Gran can you rap? Can you rap? Can you Gran?
And she opened one eye and said to me, Man,
I'm the best rapping Gran this world's ever seen
I'm a tip-top, slip-slap, rap-rap queen.

And she rose from her chair in the corner of the room
And she started to rap with a bim-bam-boom,
And she rolled up her eyes and she rolled round her
    head
And as she rolled by this is what she said.
I'm the best rapping Gran this world's ever seen
I'm a nip-nap, yip-yap, rap-rap queen.

Then she rapped past my dad and she rapped past my
    mother,
She rapped past me and my little baby brother,
She rapped her arms narrow she rapped her arms wide,
She rapped through the door and she rapped outside.
She's the best rapping Gran this world's ever seen
She's a drip-drop, trip-trap, rap-rap queen.

She rapped down the garden she rapped down the
    street,
The neighbours all cheered and they tapped their feet.
She rapped through the traffic lights as they turned red

As she rapped round the corner this is what she said,
I'm the best rapping Gran this world's ever seen
I'm a flip-flop, hip-hop, rap-rap queen.

She rapped down the lane, she rapped up the hill,
And as she disappeared she was rapping still.
I could hear Gran's voice saying, Listen, Man,
Listen to the rapping of the rap-rap Gran.
I'm the best rapping Gran this world's ever seen
I'm a –
tip-top, slip-slap,
nip-nap, yip-yap,
hip-hop, trip-trap,
touch yer cap,
take a nap,
happy, happy, happy, happy,
rap-rap-queen.

Jack Ousbey

My Gran

My gran is
a giggle-in-the-corner-like-a-child
kind of gran

She is
a put-your-cold-hand-in-my-pocket
a keep-your-baby-curls-in-my-locket
kind of gran

She is
a make-it-better-with-a-treacle-toffee
a what-you-need's-a-cup-of-milky-coffee
a hurry-home-I-love-you-awfully
kind of gran

She is
a butter-ball-for-your-bad-throat
a stitch-your-doll-a-new-green-coat
a let's-make-soapy-bubbles-float
a hold-my-hand-I'm-seasick-in-a-boat
kind of gran

She is
a toast-your-tootsies-by-the-fire
a crack-the-wishbone-for-your-heart's-desire
a ladies-don't-sweat-they-perspire
a funny-old-fashioned-higgledy-piggledy-
lady-to-admire
kind of gran

And this lovely grandmother
is mine, all mine!

Moira Andrew

I Remember, I Remember

I remember, I remember,
The house where I was born,
The little window where the sun
Came peeping in at morn;
He never came a wink too soon,
Nor brought too long a day,
But now, I often wish the night
Had borne my breath away.

I remember, I remember,
The roses, red and white;
The violets, and the lily-cups,
Those flowers made of light!
The lilacs where the robin built,
And where my brother set
The laburnum on his birthday –
The tree is living yet!

I remember, I remember,
Where I was used to swing;
And thought the air must rush as fresh
To swallows on the wing:
My spirit flew in feathers then,
That is so heavy now,
And summer pools could hardly cool
The fever on my brow!

I remember, I remember,
The fir trees dark and high;
I used to think their slender tops
Were close against the sky:
It was a childish ignorance,
But now 'tis little joy
To know I'm farther off from Heav'n
Than when I was a boy.

Thomas Hood

A Girl

A girl in our class has a faraway look.
Head in the clouds. Nose in a book.
Tiptoes around. The soles of her feet
are raw from the playground's heat.

A girl in our class has an artist's eye.
Views the world in black and white.
Open and shut. Her wide eye blinks.
Sharpens her pencil. Thinks.

A girl in our class has pale, thin skin.
Bones of a bird. Heart on a string.
She's over there – in the shade of a tree.
Won't come down until three.

Rachel Rooney

Best Friends

Would a best friend
Eat your last sweet
Talk about you behind your back
Have a party and not ask you?

Mine did.

Would a best friend
Borrow your bike without telling you
Deliberately forget your birthday
Avoid you whenever possible?

Mine did.

Would a best friend
Turn up on your bike
Give you a whole packet of your favourite sweets
Look you in the eye?

Mine did.

Would a best friend say
Sorry I talked about you behind your back
Sorry I had a party and didn't invite you
Sorry I deliberately forgot your birthday
– I thought you'd fallen out with me

Mine did.

And would a best friend say, simply,
Never mind
That's OK

I did

Bernard Young

Class Photograph

Everyone's smiling, grinning, beaming,
Even Clare Biggs who was really scheming
How she was going to get revenge
On her ex-best friend, Selina Penge
(Front row, third left, with hair in wisps)
For stealing her salt and vinegar crisps.

And Martin Layton-Smith is beaming,
Though he was almost certainly dreaming
Of warlock warriors in dripping caves
Sending mindless orcs to their gruesome graves.
(Next to him, Christopher Jordan's dream
Has something to do with a football team.)

And Ann-Marie Struthers is sort of beaming,
Though a minute ago her eyes were streaming
Because she'd been put in the second back row
And separated from Jennifer Snow.
And Jennifer Snow is beaming too,
Though Miss Bell wouldn't let her go to the loo.

And Miss Bell, yes even Miss Bell is beaming,
Though only just now we'd heard her screaming
At the boy beside her, Robert Black,
Who kept on peeling his eyelids back
And making a silly hooting noise
(Though he said that was one of the other boys).

Eve Rice is doing her best at beaming.
Yes, Eve is reasonably cheerful-seeming,
Though I think she was jealous because Ruth Chubb
Had – at last! – let me into their special club.
(In order to join the club, said Ruth,
You had to have lost at least one tooth.)

And look, that's me, and my teeth are gleaming
Around my new gap; yes, I'm *really* beaming.

Julia Donaldson

Mister Moore

Mister Moore, Mister Moore
Creaking down the corridor.

Uh uh eh eh uh
Uh uh eh eh uh

Mister Moore wears wooden suits
Mister Moore's got great big boots
Mister Moore's got hair like a brush
And Mister Moore don't like me much.

Mister Moore, Mister Moore
Creaking down the corridor.

Uh uh eh eh uh
Uh uh eh eh uh

When my teacher's there I haven't got a care
I can do my sums, I can do gerzinters
When Mister Moore comes through the door
Got a wooden head filled with splinters.

Mister Moore, Mister Moore
Creaking down the corridor.

Uh uh eh eh uh
Uh uh eh eh uh

Mister Moore I implore
My earholes ache, my head is sore

Don't come through that classroom door
Don't come through that classroom door.
Mister Mister, Mister Moore
He's creaking down the corridor.

Uh uh eh eh uh
Uh uh eh eh uh

Big voice, big hands
Big voice, he's a very big man
Take my advice, be good be very very nice
Be good be very very nice

To Mister Moore, Mister Moore
Creaking down the corridor.

Uh uh eh eh uh
Uh uh eh eh uh

Mister Moore wears wooden suits
Mister Moore's got great big boots
Mister Moore's got his hair like a brush
Mister Moore don't like me much

Mister Moore, Mister Moore
Creaking down the corridor.

Uh uh eh eh uh
Uh uh eh eh uh

David Harmer

Please Mrs Butler

Please Mrs Butler
This boy Derek Drew
Keeps copying my work, Miss.
What shall I do?

Go and sit in the hall, dear.
Go and sit in the sink.
Take your books on the roof, my lamb.
Do whatever you think.

Please Mrs Butler
This boy Derek Drew
Keeps taking my rubber, Miss.
What shall I do?

Keep it in your hand, dear.
Hide it up your vest.
Swallow it if you like, my love.
Do what you think is best.

Please Mrs Butler
This boy Derek Drew
Keeps calling me rude names, Miss.
What shall I do?

Lock yourself in the cupboard, dear.
Run away to sea.
Do whatever you can, my flower.
But *don't ask me*.

Allan Ahlberg

Teacher

When you teach me,
your hands bless the air
where chalk-dust sparkles.

And when you talk,
the six wives of Henry VIII
stand in the room like bridesmaids,

or the Nile drifts past the classroom window,
the Pyramids baking like giant cakes
on the playing fields.

You teach with your voice,
so a tiger prowls from a poem
and pads between desks, black and gold

in the shadow and sunlight,
or the golden apples of the sun drop
from a branch in my mind's eye.

I bow my head again
to this tattered, doodled book
and learn what love is.

Carol Ann Duffy

Geography Lesson

Our teacher told us one day he would leave
And sail across a warm blue sea
To places he had only known from maps,
And all his life had longed to be.

The house he lived in was narrow and grey
But in his mind's eye he could see
Sweet-scented jasmine clinging to the walls,
And green leaves burning on an orange tree.

He spoke of the lands he longed to visit,
Where it was never drab or cold,
And I couldn't understand why he never left,
And shook off the school's stranglehold.

Then halfway through his final term
He took ill and never returned,
And he never got to that place on the map
Where the green leaves of the orange trees burned.

The maps were redrawn on the classroom wall;
His name was forgotten, it faded away,
But a lesson he never knew he taught
Is with me to this day.

I travel to where the green leaves burn,
To where the ocean's glass-clear and blue,
To places our teacher taught me to love –
But which he never knew.

Brian Patten

Do You Know My Teacher?

(fill in the word you think is most appropriate)

She's got a piercing stare
and long black ...

a) *teeth*
b) *shoes*
c) *moustache*
d) *hair*
e) *earlobes*

She eats chips and beef
and has short sharp ...

a) *doorstoppers*
b) *fangs*
c) *ears*
d) *teef*
e) *moonbeams*

She is slinky and thin
and has a pointed ...

a) *banana*
b) *chin*
c) *beard*
d) *gorilla*
e) *yacht*

She has a very long nose
and hairy little ...

a) *kneecaps*
b) *paper clips*
c) *children*
d) *toes*
e) *ornaments*

She has sparkling eyes
and eats pork . . .

a) buses
b) ties
c) pies
d) thumbs
e) footballers

She comes from down south
and has a great big . . .

a) light bulb
b) egg-cup
c) vocabulary
d) piano
e) mouth

She yells like a preacher
yes, that's my . . .

a) budgie
b) stick
c) padlock
d) duckling
e) teacher

John Rice

I Think My Teacher's Wonderful

I think my teacher's wonderful,
I think my teacher's ace;
she brightens up the classroom and
she lights up every face.

Her lessons are so special,
they're a pleasure to attend;
she makes the days so memorable
I wish they'd never end.

She truly is astonishing,
a jewel that's very rare;
a unique individual
who's quite beyond compare.

Of all the teachers in the school
my teacher rates the best —
at least that's what I'll tell her
just before she grades my test.

Graham Denton

This Is Our School

This is our school
These are our friends
The journey that starts here
Will never end

This is our school
A place where we can grow
Where teachers can teach us
Things we need to know

Here we learn to read and write
Here we learn to share and play
Here we learn together
Day by day, day by day

Here we learn all the lessons
That will help us on our way
Through the years, we are here
Day by day, day by day

This is our school
For you and for me
A place we can wish
A place we can dream

This is our school
Full of memories
Classrooms of knowledge
And discovery

67

Here we learn to read and write
Here we learn to share and play
Here we learn together
Day by day, day by day

Here we learn all the lessons
That will help us on our way
Through the years, we are here
Day by day, day by day

The days they turn to weeks
The weeks they turn to years
We may pass on through
But our school is always here

Here we learn to read and write
Here we learn to share and play
Here we learn together
Day by day, day by day

Here we learn all the lessons
That will help us on our way
Through the years, we are here
Day by day, day by day

This is our school
More than these walls
We are the school
For one and for all

Paul Cookson, Stan Cullimore and Henry Priestman

Word of a Lie

I am the fastest runner in my school and that's
   NO WORD OF A LIE
I've got gold fillings in my teeth and that's
   NO WORD OF A LIE
In my garden, I've got my own big bull and that's
   NO WORD OF A LIE
I'm brilliant at giving my enemies grief and that's
   NO WORD OF A LIE
I can multiply three billion and twenty-seven by nine
      billion
four thousand and one in two seconds and that's
   NO WORD OF A LIE
I can calculate the distance between planets before
      you've
had toast and that's
   NO WORD OF A LIE
I can always tell when my best pals boast and that's
   NO WORD OF A LIE
I'd been round the world twice before I was three and a
      quarter and that's
   NO WORD OF A LIE
I am definitely my mother's favourite daughter and
      that's
   NO WORD OF A LIE
I am brilliant at fake laughter. I go Ha aha Ha ha ha
      and that's
   NO WORD OF A LIE

I can tell the weather from one look at the sky and that's
   NO WORD OF A LIE
I can predict disasters, floods, earthquakes and
      murders
and that's
   NO WORD OF A LIE
I can always tell when other people lie and that's
   NO WORD OF A LIE
I can even tell if someone is going to die and that's
   NO WORD OF A LIE
I am the most popular girl in my entire school and
      that's
   NO WORD OF A LIE
I know the golden rule, don't play the fool, don't boast,
      be
shy and that's
   NO WORD OF A LIE
I am sensitive, I listen, I have kind brown eyes and
      that's
   NO WORD OF A LIE

You don't believe me do you?
ALL RIGHT, ALL RIGHT, ALL RIGHT
I am the biggest liar in my school and that's
   NO WORD OF A LIE

Jackie Kay

Secret

Tell me your secret.
I promise not to tell.
I'll guard it safely at the bottom of a well.

Tell me your secret
Tell me, tell me, please.
I won't breathe a word, not even to the bees.

Tell me your secret.
It will be a pebble in my mouth.
Not even the sea can make me spit it out.

John Agard

Our Tree

It takes so long for a tree to grow
So many years of pushing the sky.
Long branches stretch their arms
Reach out with their wooden fingers.
Years drift by, fall like leaves
From green to yellow then back to green.
Since my grandad was a boy
And then before his father's father
There's been an elm outside our school
Its shadow long across the playground.
Today three men ripped it down.
Chopped it up. It took ten minutes.

David Harmer

Timothy Winters

Timothy Winters comes to school
With eyes as wide as a football pool,
Ears like bombs and teeth like splinters:
A blitz of a boy is Timothy Winters.

His belly is white, his neck is dark,
And his hair is an exclamation mark.
His clothes are enough to scare a crow
And through his britches the blue winds blow.

When teacher talks he won't hear a word
And he shoots down dead the arithmetic-bird,
He licks the pattern off his plate
And he's not even heard of the Welfare State.

Timothy Winters has bloody feet
And he lives in a house on Suez Street,
He sleeps in a sack on the kithen floor
And they say there aren't boys like him any more.

Old Man Winters likes his beer
And his missus ran off with a bombardier,
Grandma sits in the grate with a gin
And Timothy's dosed with an aspirin.

The Welfare Worker lies awake
But the law's as tricky as a ten-foot snake,
So Timothy Winters drinks his cup
And slowly goes on growing up.

At Morning Prayers the Master helves
For children less fortunate than ourselves,
And the loudest response in the room is when
Timothy Winters roars 'Amen!'

So come one angel, come on ten:
Timothy Winters says 'Amen
Amen amen amen amen.'
Timothy Winters, Lord.

Amen

Charles Causley

Four O' Clock Friday

Four o'clock Friday, I'm home at last.
Time to forget the week that's past.
On Monday, in break they stole my ball
And threw it over the playground wall.
On Tuesday afternoon, in games
They threw mud at me and called me names.
On Wednesday, they trampled my books on the floor
So Miss kept me in because I swore.
On Thursday, they laughed after the test
'Cause my marks were lower than the rest.
Four o'clock Friday, at last I'm free,
For two whole days they can't get at me.

John Foster

The Things Around You

Make use of the things around you,
suggested Raymond Carver –
the man sitting opposite me
on the 5.15 to Leicester sips sweet tea.
His styrofoam cup sweats.
The Twix bar glitters false bronze.
Water bubbles in my lemonade rise and pop.
The tap of computers by commuters
punctuates the train's rumble.
The low hum of conversation
and awkward glances pass the time.
A mum leans forwards to swap gossip with her
daughter;
both dressed in tank tops and jeans
they address their faces; stroking their darkening
eyebrows.
Reflections ghost the train window;
my mirror image gazes back.
Beyond, the black river slides by.
Towns glide past like dark swans.
Road lights are bright-orange necklaces.
A motorway becomes an artery.

Wellingborough station is a cold shadow.
Passengers pace, restless with waiting.
The display board marks time and I'm
making the most of the 5.15 to Leicester,
carving up the things around me.

Pie Corbett

Adult Fiction

I always loved libraries, the quiet of them,
The smell of the plastic covers and the paper
And the tables and the silence of them,
The silence of them that if you listened wasn't silence,
It was the murmur of stories held for years on shelves
And the soft clicking of the date stamp,
The soft clickety-clicking of the date stamp.

I used to go down to our little library on a Friday night
In late summer, just as autumn was thinking about
Turning up, and the light outside would be the colour
Of an Everyman cover and the lights in the library
Would be soft as anything, and I'd sit at a table
And flick through a book and fall in love
With the turning of the leaves, the turning of the
    leaves.

And then at seven o'clock Mrs Dove would say
In a voice that wasn't too loud so it wouldn't
Disturb the books 'Seven o'clock please . . .'
And as I was the only one in the library's late summer
    rooms
I would be the only one to stand up and close my book
And put it back on the shelf with a sound like a kiss,
Back on the shelf with a sound like a kiss.

And I'd go out of the library and Mrs Dove would stand
For a moment silhouetted by the Adult Fiction,
And then she would turn the light off and lock the door
And go to her little car and drive off into the night
That was slowly turning the colour of ink and I would
  stand
For two minutes and then I'd walk over to the dark
  library
And just stand in front of the dark library.

Ian McMillan

Everything Touches

Everything touches, life interweaves
Starlight and wood-smoke, ashes and leaves
Birdsong and thunder, acid and rain
Everything touches, unbroken chain

Rainstorm and rainbow, warrior and priest
Stingray and dolphin, beauty and beast
Heartbeat and high tide, ebb tide and flow
The universe in a crystal of snow

Snowdrop and death-cap, hangman and clown
Walls that divide come tumbling down
Seen through the night, the glimmer of day
Life is but darkness worn away

Blackness and whiteness, sunset and dawn
Those gone before, yet to be born
Past and future, distance and time
Atom to atom, water to wine

Look all around and what do you see?
Everything touches, you're touching me
Look all around and what do you see?
Everything touches, you're touching me.

Roger McGough

Reading the Classics

The Secret Garden will never age;
The tangled undergrowth remains as fresh
As when the author put down her pen.
It's mysteries are as poignant now as then.

Though Time's a thief it cannot thieve
One page from the world of make-believe.

On the track the Railway Children wait;
Alice still goes back and forth through the glass;
In Tom's Midnight Garden Time unfurls,
And children still discover secret worlds.

At the Gates of Dawn Pan plays his pipes;
Mole and Ratty still float in awe downstream.
The weasels watch, hidden in the grass.
None cares how quickly human years pass.

Though Time's a thief it cannot thieve
One page from the world of make-believe.

Brian Patten

Take a Poem

Why not take a poem
wherever you go?
pop it in your pocket
nobody will know

Take it to your classroom
stick it on the wall
tell them all about it
read it in the hall

Take it to the bathroom
tuck it up in bed
take the time to learn it
keep it in your head

Take it for a day trip
take it on a train
fold it as a hat
when it starts to rain

Take it to a river
fold it as a boat
pop it in the water
hope that it will float

Take it to a hilltop
fold it as a plane
throw it up skywards
time and time again

Take it to a post box
send it anywhere
out into the world with
tender
loving
care

James Carter

I Like Words

I like words.
Do you like words?
Words aren't hard to find:
Words on walls and words in books,
Words deep in your mind.

Words in jokes
That make you laugh,
Words that seem to smell.
Words that end up inside out,
Words you cannot spell.

Words that fly
And words that crawl,
Words that screech and bump.
Words that glide and words that swing,
Words that bounce and jump.

Words that paint
And words that draw,
Words that make you grin.
Words that make you shake and sweat,
Words that touch your skin.

Words of love
That keep you warm,
Words that make you glad.
Words that hit you, words that hurt,
Words that make you sad.

Words in French
And words in slang,
Words like 'guy' and 'dude'.
Words you make up, words you steal,
Words they say are rude.

I like words.
Do you like words?
Words come out and play.
Words are free and words are friends,
Words are great to say.

Steve Turner

The Sound Collector

A stranger called this morning
Dressed all in black and grey
Put every sound into a bag
And carried them away

The whistling of the kettle
The turning of the lock
The purring of the kitten
The ticking of the clock

The popping of the toaster
The crunching of the flakes
When you spread the marmalade
The scraping noise it makes

The hissing of the frying pan
The ticking of the grill
The bubbling of the bathtub
As it starts to fill

The drumming of the raindrops
On the windowpane
When you do the washing-up
The gurgle of the drain

The crying of the baby
The squeaking of the chairs
The swishing of the curtains
The creaking of the stairs

A stranger called this morning
He didn't leave his name
Left us only silence
Life will never be the same.

Roger McGough

Forbidden Poem

This poem is not for children.
Keep out!
There is a big oak door
in front of this poem.
It's locked.
And on the door is a notice
in big red letters.
It says: any child who enters here
will never be the same again.
WARNING. KEEP OUT.

But what's this?
A key in the keyhole.
And what's more,
nobody's about.

'Go on, look,'
says a little voice
inside your head.
'Surely a poem
cannot strike you dead?'

You turn the key.
The door swings wide.
And then you witness
what's inside.

And from that day
you'll try in vain.
You'll never be the same again.

Tony Mitton

Some Favourite Words

Mugwump, chubby, dunk and whoa,
Swizzle, doom and snoop,
Flummox, lilt and afterglow,
Gruff, bamboozle, whoop
And nincompoop.

Wallow, jungle, lumber, sigh,
Ooze and zodiac,
Innuendo, lullaby,
Ramp and mope and quack
And paddywhack.

Moony, undone, lush and bole,
Inkling, tusk, guffaw,
Waspish, croon and cubby-hole,
Fern, fawn, dumbledore
And many more . . .

Worm.

Richard Edwards

Wurd Up

Blowin like a hurricane
Destroyin all the competishan
Kickin up the lirix hard
There ain't no opposishan
Coz
Wen I'm on a roll like this
I'm jus like a physishan
Like a boxer . . . punch you out
With lirical precishan
Flowing like a river
Jus
Flyin like a bird
'n'
Checkin out the ridim
Jus
In my wurdz
It's time
Ter climb
'n' rime
The sign
Jus grows
'n' flows
'n' shows
'n' throws
A skill
Ter thrill
'n' kill
Just chill

Coz I'm
Stingin like a nettle
Just bitin like a flea
Smoother than a baby's skin
Much ruffer than the sea
Colder than an icicle
Hotter than the sun
Lirix always on the move
Like bullets from a gun
Much noisier than thunder
Much cooler than the rain
I'm fitter than an exercise
Deep within the brain
Sharper than a needle
More solid than a rock
Repeatin like an echo
As rhythmic as a clock
More dangerus than a lion
Much louder than a plane
As quiet as a whisper
I burn yer like a flame
Faster than a jaguar
Slower than a snail
Yeah! rapid like a heartbeat
Tuffer than a nail

More painful than a scratch
As tasty as food
Horrible like a medicine
My lirix change yer mood
As tasty as a mango
As bitter as a lime
Softer than a coconut
Endless as the time
Kickin like a raggae song
Much sadder than the blues
I'm as tirin as a marathon
Give yer all the news
Wilder than a stampede
As gentle as a breeze
Irritatin as a cough
More wicked than a sneeze
More lively than a child
Romantic that's me
Still harsh like the winter
Just buzzin like a bee
The rimes 'n' times are signs
To blow 'n' show a flow
The wurdz
WURD UP!

Martin Glynn

What a Poem's Not

A poem is not an Ant
but it can be quite short.
A poem is not a Banana
but there may be something under its skin.
A poem is not a Coat
but it may have some warmth in it.
A poem is not a Dog
but it might be quite a friend.
A poem is not an Endless pair of trousers
but it can be quite long.
A poem is not a Football
shaped like a cucumber.
A poem is not a Great
number of things.
A poem is not a Hedgehog
but it might be hard to get hold of.
A poem is not an Igloo
but it can feel like home.
A poem is not a Jumble sale
but it might contain some rubbish.
A poem is not a Kite
but it might enjoy the wind.
A poem is not a Light bulb
but you can change it if you want to.
A poem is not a Monkey
but it can be quite human.
A poem is not a Nut
but you can give it to a monkey.

A poem is not a Opera score or an open score
but it can be revealing.
A poem is not a Prison
and it shouldn't feel like one either.
A poem is not a Question . . .
actually it is sometimes.
A poem is not a Radio
but you may have to tune in to it.
A poem is not a Slot machine
but you may have to put something into it.
A poem is not a Toothbrush
so don't clean your teeth with it.
A poem is not a Umbrella
but it can give you protection.
A poem is not a Verruca
and I'm glad.
A poem is not a Wig
but maybe it will change you.
A poem is not an X-ray
make no bones about it.
A poem is not a Year-old bag of vegetables
but it can smell quite strongly.
A poem is not a Zylophone
and it can spell words wrongly.

John Hegley

We Are the Writers

We are readers, we are writers
We love to share the words that excite us

We are poets, we are singers
We love to share the melodies they bring us

We are actors, we are dancers
We love to have the questions and the answers

It only takes one spark to start the fire
Just one idea to inspire
It only takes one dream to take you higher

It only takes one voice to breathe these words
So they live and so they can be heard
These lines and these rhymes will give the world
So many writers

We are searchers, we are seekers
Where there are secrets, we are the keepers

We are doers, we are makers
We are the movers, we are the shakers

We are thinkers, we are dreamers
We are here because we are believers ...

It only takes one spark to start the fire
Just one idea to inspire
It only takes one dream to take you higher

It only takes one voice to breathe these words
So they live and so they can be heard
These lines and these rhymes will give the world
So many writers

We are readers, we are writers
We love to share the words that excite us

We are the writers

Paul Cookson

Thought Cloud

Throw a rope 'round a cloud
heave it on down –
what might be found inside?

a fallen angel's wing
a postcard from the wind
a torn red kite
pieces of the night

an air hostess's nail
frozen vapour trails
a pterodactyl's tooth
a parachute's whoosh

a solid silver harp
one dark star
a lock of moon-white hair
and
a pilot's last prayer

Matt Goodfellow

List of Lists

I love making lists so much
I've made a list of lists

Shopping list
Things-to-do-today list
List of best friends you can count on
List of friends whose shoulder you can cry on
Top-ten list of fast-food places
List of gruesome punishments
List of favourite excuses
List of favourite Olympic races
List of ingredients for giant pizza
List of wishes in case a magic genie appears
List of favourite words that rhyme
Sir Bobby Robson and Sir Alex Ferguson (List of knights)
Bewildered. Shell-shocked. Confused (List of daze)
List of presents wanted at Christmas time
List of things to do tomorrow
And number one on tomorrow's list is . . . ?
Make a new list

Roger Stevens

The Magic Box

I will put in the box ...

the swish of a silk sari on a summer night,
fire from the nostrils of a Chinese dragon,
the tip of a tongue touching a tooth.

I will put in the box ...

a snowman with a rumbling belly,
a sip of the bluest water from Lake Lucerne,
a leaping spark from an electric fish.

I will put into the box ...

three violet wishes spoken in Gujarati,
the last joke of an ancient uncle
and the first smile of a baby.

I will put into the box ...

a fifth season and a black sun,
a cowboy on a broomstick
and a witch on a white horse.

My box is fashioned from ice and gold and steel,
with stars on the lid and secrets in the corners.
Its hinges are the toe joints of dinosaurs.

I shall surf in my box
on the great high-rolling breakers of the wild Atlantic,
then wash ashore on a yellow beach
the colour of the sun.

Kit Wright

The Land of Story-books

At evening when the lamp is lit,
Around the fire my parents sit;
They sit at home and talk and sing,
And do not play at anything.

Now, with my little gun, I crawl
All in the dark along the wall,
And follow round the forest track
Away behind the sofa back.

There, in the night, where none can spy,
All in my hunter's camp I lie,
And play at books that I have read
Till it is time to go to bed.

These are the hills, these are the woods,
These are my starry solitudes;
And there the river by whose brink
The roaring lions come to drink.

I see the others far away
As if in firelit camp they lay,
And I, like to an Indian scout,
Around their party prowled about.

So, when my nurse comes in for me,
Home I return across the sea,
And go to bed with backward looks
At my dear land of Story-books.

Robert Louis Stevenson

How Many?

How many seconds in a minute?
Sixty, and no more in it.

How many minutes in an hour?
Sixty for sun and shower.

How many hours in a day?
Twenty-four for work and play.

How many days in a week?
Seven both to hear and speak.

How many weeks in a month?
Four, as the swift moon runn'th.

How many months in a year?
Twelve the almanack makes clear.

How many years in an age?
One hundred says the sage.

How many ages in time?
No one knows the rhyme.

Christina Rossetti

1 Do as Simon Says

I'm nobody's dog but Simon's
I do as Simon says,
If Simon said, 'Delilah, dance!'
I'd be up on my two hind legs.

But Simon says, 'Delilah, sit!'
He says, 'Delilah, stay!'
Yet if he said, 'Delilah, sing!'
I'd somehow find a way.

I'm nobody's dog but Simon's,
I do as Simon says,
He sometimes says, 'Delilah, fetch!'
And I save Simon's legs.

But Simon is no tyrant,
He takes me out for walks,
I always keep one step ahead
And listen as he talks.

My watchword is Obedience,
And Simon's love, my prize,
We go together everywhere
For I am Simon's eyes.

Celia Warren

The Mouse and the Lion

In the hottest sun of the longest day
A lion lay down for a doze.
A little brown mouse pattered out to play.
He danced on the whiskery nose.
Pit-a-pat, pit-a-pat, pit-a-pat, pit-a-pat,
He danced on the whiskery nose.

The lion awoke with a sneeze, 'A-choo!'
He picked up the mouse in his paw.
'And who may I venture to ask are you?'
He said with a terrible roar.
Grr, grrr, grrrrr, GRRRRRR,
He said with a terrible roar.

'I'll save your life if you'll let me go.'
The mouse's voice shook as he spoke.
The lion laughed loudly, 'Oh ho ho ho.
I'll let you go free for your joke.'
Oho, oho, ohohohoho,
I'll let you go free for your joke.

As chance would have it, the following week
The lion was caught in a net
When all of a sudden he heard a squeak:
'Well met, noble lion, well met.'
Squeak, squeak, squeak, squeak,
Well met, noble lion, well met.

The little mouse nibbled and gnawed and bit
Till the lion was finally free.
'It's nothing, dear lion, don't mention it:
I'm repaying your kindness to me.'
Nibbly, nibbly, nibbly, nibble,
Repaying your kindness to me.

'For one of the lessons which mice must learn
From their whiskery father and mother
Is the famous old saying that one good turn
Always deserves another.'
Pit-a-pat, grrr, ohoho, squeak!
Always deserves another.

Julia Donaldson

Walking with My Iguana

*(words in brackets to be replaced by another voice
or voices)*

I'm walking (I'm walking)
with my iguana (with my iguana)

I'm walking (I'm walking)
with my iguana (with my iguana)

When the temperature rises
to above eighty-five,
my iguana is looking
like he's coming alive

So we make it to the beach,
my iguana and me,
then he sits on my shoulder
as we stroll by the sea ...

and I'm walking (I'm walking)
with my iguana (with my iguana)

I'm walking (I'm walking)
with my iguana (with my iguana)

Well if anyone sees us
we're a big surprise,
my iguana and me
on our daily exercise,

till somebody phones
the local police
and says I have an alligator
tied to a leash

when I'm walking (I'm walking)
with my iguana (with my iguana)

I'm walking (I'm walking)
with my iguana (with my iguana)

It's the spines on his back
that make him look grim,
but he just loves to be tickled
under his chin.

And my iguana will tell me
that he's ready for bed
when he puts on his pyjamas
and lays down his sleepy (yawn) head.

And I'm walking (I'm walking)
with my iguana (with my iguana)

still walking (still walking)
with my iguana (with my iguana)

With my iguana . . .

with my iguana . . .

and my piranha . . .

and my chihuahua ...

and my chinchilla,

with my groovy gorilla ...

my caterpillar ...

and I'm walking ...

with my iguana ...

Brian Moses

from I Think I Could Turn and Live with Animals

I think I could turn and live with animals, they are so
    placid and self-contained;
I stand and look at them long and long.
They do not sweat and whine about their condition;
They do not lie awake in the dark and weep for their
    sins;
They do not make me sick discussing their duty to
    God;
Not one is dissatisfied – not one is demented with the
    mania of owning things;
Not one kneels to another, nor to his kind that lived
    thousands of years ago;
Not one is respectable or industrious over the whole
    earth.

Walt Whitman

The Eagle

He clasps the crag with crooked hands;
Close to the sun in lonely lands,
Ringed with the azure world, he stands.

The wrinkled sea beneath him crawls;
He watches from his mountain walls,
And like a thunderbolt he falls.

Alfred, Lord Tennyson

Let There Be Peace

Let there be peace
So frowns fly away like an albatross
And skeletons foxtrot from cupboards;
So war correspondents become travel-show presenters
And magpies bring back lost property,
Children, engagement rings, broken things.

Let there be peace
So storms can go out to sea to be
Angry and return to me calm;
So the broken can rise and dance in the hospitals.
Let the aged Ethiopian man in the grey block of flats
Peer through his window and see Addis before him
So his thrilled outstretched arms become frames
For his dreams.

Let there be peace
Let tears evaporate to form clouds, cleanse themselves
And fall into reservoirs of drinking water.
Let harsh memories burst into fireworks that melt
In the dark pupils of a child's eyes
And disappear like shoals of darting silver fish.
And let the waves reach the shore with
Shhhhhhhhhh shhhhhhhhhh shhhhhhhhhh

Lemn Sissay

If—

If you can keep your head when all about you
Are losing theirs and blaming it on you,
If you can trust yourself when all men doubt you,
But make allowance for their doubting too;
If you can wait and not be tired by waiting,
Or being lied about, don't deal in lies,
Or being hated, don't give way to hating,
And yet don't look too good, nor talk too wise:

If you can dream—and not make dreams your master;
If you can think—and not make thoughts your aim;
If you can meet with Triumph and Disaster
And treat those two impostors just the same;
If you can bear to hear the truth you've spoken
Twisted by knaves to make a trap for fools,
Or watch the things you gave your life to, broken,
And stoop and build 'em up with worn-out tools:

If you can make one heap of all your winnings
And risk it on one turn of pitch-and-toss,
And lose, and start again at your beginnings
And never breathe a word about your loss;
If you can force your heart and nerve and sinew
To serve your turn long after they are gone,
And so hold on when there is nothing in you
Except the Will which says to them: 'Hold on!'

If you can talk with crowds and keep your virtue,
Or walk with Kings—nor lose the common touch,
If neither foes nor loving friends can hurt you,
If all men count with you, but none too much;
If you can fill the unforgiving minute
With sixty seconds' worth of distance run,
Yours is the Earth and everything that's in it,
And—which is more—you'll be a Man, my son!

Rudyard Kipling

People Equal

Some people shoot up tall.
Some hardly leave the ground at all.
Yet – people equal. Equal.

One voice is a sweet mango.
Another is a non-sugar tomato.
Yet – people equal. Equal.

Some people rush to the front.
Others hang back, feeling they can't.
Yet – people equal. Equal.

Hammer some people, you meet a wall.
Blow hard on others they fall.
Yet – people equal. Equal.

One person will aim at a star.
For another, a hilltop is *too far*.
Yet – people equal. Equal.

Some people get on with their show.
Others never get on the go.
Yet – people equal. Equal.

James Berry

Body Talk

Dere's a Sonnet
Under me bonnet
Dere's a Epic
In me ear,
Dere's a Novel
In me navel
Dere's a Classic
Here somewhere.
Dere's a Movie
In me left knee
A long story
In me right,
Dere's a shorty
Inbetweeny
It is tickly
In de night.
Dere's a picture
In me ticker
Unmixed riddims
In me heart,
In me texture
Dere's a comma
In me fat chin
Dere is Art.

Dere's an Opera
In me bladder
A Ballad's
In me wrist,
Dere is laughter
In me shoulder
In me guzzard's
A nice twist.
In me dreadlocks
Dere is syntax
A dance kicks
In me bum,
Thru me blood tracks
Dere run true facts
I got limericks
From me Mum,
Documentaries
In me entries
Plays on history
In me folk,
Dere's a Trilogy
When I tink of three
On me toey
Dere's a joke.

Benjamin Zephaniah

Give Yourself a Hug

Give yourself a hug
when you feel unloved

Give yourself a hug
when people put on airs
to make you feel a bug

Give yourself a hug
when everyone seems to give you
a cold-shoulder shrug

Give yourself a hug –
a big big hug

And keep on singing,
'Only one in a million like me
Only one in a million-billion-thrillion-zillion
like me.'

Grace Nichols

If I Could Choose

If I could choose the gifts
that life would give to me,
what choices would I make,
and just who would I be?

I wouldn't choose fast cars
being friends with all the stars.
I wouldn't choose to sign an autograph.
I wouldn't choose to rule the sky
be superman or to fly.
I wouldn't choose to cry – when I could laugh.

I wouldn't choose fame
people calling out my name.
I wouldn't choose pots and pots of money.
I wouldn't choose to be the best
or be brighter than the rest
although I wouldn't mind being funny.

I wouldn't choose football
or any sport at all.
I wouldn't choose big muscles for a fight.
I wouldn't choose pride of place
or to have the prettiest face.
I wouldn't choose the wrong – instead of right.

If I could choose the gifts
that life could give to me,
I'd choose good friends, good health
and ... my family.

But win or lose,
I would choose,
to just
be
ME.

Stan Cullimore

Future Masterpiece

If we could paint the future
And hang it in a frame,
From that moment onwards
The world would never be the same.

We would recycle paper
And turn it back into trees.
Turn honey into pollen
And feed it to the bees.

We'd throw war out the window
And watch it shatter on the floor.
Prise open the door of understanding
Hypnotize the rich to give to the poor.

There'd be a children's parliament
We'd sit and discuss issues of the day.
Adults who refused to listen
Would be kept in during play.

If we could paint the future
And hang it in a frame,
From that moment onwards
The world would never be the same.

The earth would be seen as sacred
The rainforest a holy shrine.
Caretakers for a season
No one could say, 'That piece of land is mine.'

We'd invent new ways of travelling
Flying cars that ran on fresh air.
We'd have robots to do the cleaning
We'd call them Bush-extractor and grizzly-Blair.

Racism would dissolve like snow
When zapped by truth rays from the sun.
Martin Luther King's dream would be complete
When there's respect for everyone.

If we could paint the future
And hang it in a frame,
From that moment onwards
The world would never be the same.

We humans would create a new religion
We'd call it giving back so we can live.
Its focus would not be receiving
It would be based on what you can give.

The future is a present
Unwrapped in a different time,
Swaddled in the past
The future is yours and mine.

If we could paint the future
And hang it in a frame,
From that moment onwards
The world would never be the same.

Adisa

Think Big

Crossing borderlines with broader rhymes
I generate ideas that blow your mind
You see my awesome mind does more than rhyme
I'm thinking all the time with thoughts of mine
My thoughts are 3D and HD all combined
Sharper than the spines on a porcupine
Signed, sealed and delivery is – full of imagery
Vividly visualized through my eyes, spoken terrifically
I'm so unique; my own shadow can't even mimic me
My visions make me think into infinity
Do things differently with authenticity
And aim high specifically
Cos inside of you and inside of me
There's a genius inside that no one can see
Do you know what you want and who you wanna be?
We're bigger than we think but it's hard to see
Fling your mind to the edge of the world ... now bring
   it back
Think outside the box and in your thinking cap
Dream bigger than you think your dreams can be
Open up your mind's eye so it can see
Possible impossibilities
Unlimited things to achieve so don't be limited
Or prohibited from getting into it
My intuition is telling me your ambition is big
Don't let people get you mad, get even
Always think big and believe in
Your ability to do things you thought you couldn't

You might think you can't but really you shouldn't
Cos inside of you and inside of me
There's a genius inside that no one can see
Do you know what you want and who you want to be?
We're bigger than we think but it's hard to see

Breis

May You Always

May your smile be ever present
May your skies always be blue
May your path be ever onward
May your heart be ever true

May your dreams be full to bursting
May your steps always be sure
May the fire within your soul
Blaze on for evermore

May you live to meet ambition
May you strive to pass each test
May you find the love your life deserves
May you always have the best

May your happiness be plentiful
May your regrets be few
May you always be my best friend
May you always be . . . just you

Paul Cookson

Jabberwocky

'Twas brillig, and the slithy toves
Did gyre and gimble in the wabe;
All mimsy were the borogoves,
And the mome raths outgrabe.

'Beware the Jabberwock, my son!
The jaws that bite, the claws that catch!
Beware the Jubjub bird, and shun
The frumious Bandersnatch!'

He took his vorpal sword in hand:
Long time the manxome foe he sought—
So rested he by the Tumtum tree,
And stood awhile in thought.

And as in uffish thought he stood,
The Jabberwock, with eyes of flame,
Came whiffling through the tulgey wood,
And burbled as it came!

One, two! One, two! And through and through
The vorpal blade went snicker-snack!
He left it dead, and with its head
He went galumphing back.

'And hast thou slain the Jabberwock?
Come to my arms, my beamish boy!
O frabjous day! Callooh! Callay!'
He chortled in his joy.

'Twas brillig, and the slithy toves
Did gyre and gimble in the wabe;
All mimsy were the borogoves,
And the mome raths outgrabe.

Lewis Carroll

Fire Burn, and Cauldron Bubble

Round about the cauldron go;
In the poison'd entrails throw.
Toad, that under cold stone
Days and nights has thirty-one
Swelter'd venom, sleeping got,
Boil thou first i' the charmed pot.
Double, double toil and trouble;
Fire burn, and cauldron bubble.
Fillet of a fenny snake,
In the cauldron boil and bake;
Eye of newt, and toe of frog,
Wool of bat, and tongue of dog,
Adder's fork, and blind-worm's sting,
Lizard's leg, and owlet's wing.
For a charm of powerful trouble,
Like a hell-broth boil and bubble.
Double, double toil and trouble;
Fire burn, and cauldron bubble.

William Shakespeare

Oh, I Wish I'd Looked After Me Teeth

Oh, I wish I'd looked after me teeth,
And spotted the dangers beneath
All the toffees I chewed,
And the sweet sticky food.
Oh, I wish I'd looked after me teeth.

I wish I'd been that much more willin'
When I had more tooth there than fillin'
To give up gobstoppers,
From respect to me choppers,
And to buy something else with me shillin'.

When I think of the lollies I licked
And the liquorice allsorts I picked,
Sherbet dabs, big and little,
All that hard peanut brittle,
My conscience gets horribly pricked.

My mother, she told me no end,
If you got a tooth, you got a friend.'
I was young then, and careless,
My toothbrush was hairless,
I never had much time to spend.

Oh, I showed them the toothpaste all right,
I flashed it about late at night,
But up-and-down brushin'
And pokin' and fussin'
Didn't seem worth the time – I could bite!

If I'd known I was paving the way
To cavities, caps and decay,
The murder of fillin's,
Injections and drillin's,
I'd have thrown all me sherbet away.

So I lie in the old dentist's chair,
And I gaze up his nose in despair,
And his drill it do whine
In these molars of mine.
'Two amalgam,' he'll say, 'for in there.'

How I laughed at my mother's false teeth,
As they foamed in the waters beneath.
But now comes the reckonin'
It's me they are beckonin'
Oh, I wish I'd looked after me teeth.

Pam Ayres

The Lion and Albert

There's a famous seaside place called Blackpool,
That's noted for fresh air and fun,
And Mr and Mrs Ramsbottom
Went there with young Albert, their son.

A fine little lad was young Albert,
All dressed in his best; quite a swell.
He'd a stick with an 'orse's 'ead 'andle;
The finest that Woolworth's could sell.

They didn't think much to the ocean,
The waves they were piddlin' and small.
There was no wrecks and nobody drownded,
'Fact, nothin' to laugh at at all!

So, seeking for further amusement,
They paid, and went into the zoo,
Where they'd lions and tigers and camels
And cold ale and sandwiches too.

There were one great big lion called Wallace
Whose nose was all covered with scars;
He lay in a som-no-lent posture
With the side of his face on the bars.

Now Albert 'ad 'eard about lions –
'Ow they was ferocious and wild;
To see Wallace lyin' so peaceful
Just didn't seem right to the child.

So straight 'way the brave little feller,
Not showin' a morsel of fear,
Took 'is stick with the 'orse's 'ead 'andle
And stuck it in Wallace's ear.

You could see that the lion didn't like it,
For givin' a kind of a roll,
'E pulled Albert inside the cage with 'im
And swallered the little lad – 'ole!

Then Pa, who 'ad seen the occurrence,
And didn't know what to do next,
Said 'Mother! Yon lion's 'et Albert!'
An' Mother said 'Ee, I am vexed!'

Then Mr and Mrs Ramsbottom
Quite rightly, when all's said and done
Complained to the Animal Keeper
That the lion had eaten their son.

The keeper was quite nice about it
He said 'My, what a nasty mis'ap;
Are you sure it's your boy 'e's eaten?'
Pa said 'Am I sure? There's 'is cap!'

The manager 'ad to be sent for;
'E came and 'e said 'What's to-do?'
Pa said 'Yon lion's 'et Albert,
And 'im in 'is Sunday clothes, too!'

Then Mother said 'Right's right, young feller –
I think it's a shame and a sin
For a lion to go and eat Albert
And after we've paid to come in.'

The manager wanted no trouble;
He took out his purse right away,
Sayin' "Ow much to settle the matter?'
And Pa said 'What do you usually pay?'

But Mother 'ad turned a bit awkward
When she thought where 'er Albert 'ad gone.
She said 'No! Someone's got to be summonsed!'
So that was decided upon.

Then off they all went to the Police Station
In front of a Magistrate chap;
They told 'im what 'appened to Albert
And proved it by showing 'is cap.

The Magistrate gave 'is opinion
That no one was really to blame,
And 'e said that 'e 'oped the Ramsbottoms
Would 'ave further sons to their name.

At that Mother got proper blazin':
'And thank you, sir, kindly,' said she –
'What, waste all our lives raisin' children
To feed ruddy lions? Not me!'

Marriott Edgar

The Door

Go and open the door.
Maybe outside there's
a tree, or a wood,
a garden,
or a magic city.

Go and open the door.
Maybe a dog's rummaging.
Maybe you'll see a face,
or an eye,
or the picture
of a picture.

Go and open the door.
If there's a fog
it will clear.

Go and open the door.
Even if there's only
the darkness ticking,
even if there's only
the hollow wind,
even if
nothing
is there,
go and open the door.

At least
there'll be
a draught.

Miroslav Holub

Leisure

What is this life if, full of care,
We have no time to stand and stare?—

No time to stand beneath the boughs,
And stare as long as sheep and cows:

No time to see, when woods we pass,
Where squirrels hide their nuts in grass:

No time to see, in broad daylight,
Streams full of stars, like skies at night:

No time to turn at Beauty's glance,
And watch her feet, how they can dance:

No time to wait till her mouth can
Enrich that smile her eyes began?

A poor life this if, full of care,
We have no time to stand and stare.

W. H. Davies

Jerusalem

And did those feet in ancient time
Walk upon England's mountains green?
And was the holy Lamb of God
On England's pleasant pastures seen?

And did the countenance divine
Shine forth upon our clouded hills?
And was Jerusalem builded here
Among those dark satanic mills?

Bring me my bow of burning gold:
Bring me my arrows of desire:
Bring me my spear: O clouds unfold!
Bring me my chariot of fire.

I will not cease from mental fight,
Nor shall my sword sleep in my hand
Till we have built Jerusalem
In England's green and pleasant land.

William Blake

Christmas Market

Tall, white-haired in her widow's black
My Nana took me, balaclava'd from the cold
To where stalls shimmered in a splash of gold,
Buttery light from wind-twitched lamps and all
The Christmas hoards were heaped above my eyes,
A shrill cascade of tinsel set to fall
In a sea of shivering colours on the frosty
Foot-pocked earth. I smelt the roasted nuts
Drank syrupy sarsaparilla in thick glasses far
Too hot to hold and chewed a liquorice root
That turned into a soggy yellow brush. The man
Who wound the barrel organ let me turn
The handle and I jangled out a tune –
And Lily of Laguna spangled out into the bright night
    air
And would go on spinning through the turning years.

Then we walked home, I clutching a tin car
With half men painted on the windows, chewed a sweet
And held her hand as she warmed mine,
One glove lost turning the chattering music.
And I looked up at the circus of the stars
That spread across the city and our street
Coated now with a Christmas-cake layer of frost,
And nobody under all those stars I thought
Was a half of a half of a half as happy as me.

Mike Harding

Nativity in 20 Seconds

Silent night
Candle light
Holy bright

Stable poor
Prickly straw
Donkey snore

Babe asleep
Lambs leap
Shepherds peep

Star guide
Kings ride
Manger side

Angels wing
Bells ring
Children sing
WELCOME KING!

Coral Rumble

The Charge of the Light Brigade

Half a league, half a league,
Half a league onward,
All in the valley of Death
Rode the six hundred.
'Forward, the Light Brigade!
Charge for the guns!' he said.
Into the valley of Death
Rode the six hundred.

'Forward, the Light Brigade!'
Was there a man dismayed?
Not though the soldier knew
Some one had blundered.
Theirs not to make reply,
Theirs not to reason why,
Theirs but to do and die.
Into the valley of Death
Rode the six hundred.

Cannon to right of them,
Cannon to left of them,
Cannon in front of them
Volleyed and thundered;
Stormed at with shot and shell,
Boldly they rode and well,
Into the jaws of Death,
Into the mouth of Hell
Rode the six hundred.

Flashed all their sabres bare,
Flashed as they turned in air
Sabring the gunners there,
Charging an army, while
All the world wondered.
Plunged in the battery-smoke
Right through the line they broke;
Cossack and Russian
Reeled from the sabre-stroke
Shattered and sundered.
Then they rode back, but not,
Not the six hundred.

Cannon to right of them,
Cannon to left of them,
Cannon behind them
Volleyed and thundered;
Stormed at with shot and shell,
While horse and hero fell,
They that had fought so well
Came through the jaws of Death,
Back from the mouth of Hell,
All that was left of them,
Left of six hundred.

When can their glory fade?
O the wild charge they made!
All the world wondered.
Honour the charge they made!
Honour the Light Brigade,
Noble six hundred!

Alfred, Lord Tennyson

In Flanders Fields

In Flanders fields the poppies blow
Between the crosses, row on row,
That mark our place; and in the sky
The larks, still bravely singing, fly
Scarce heard amid the guns below.

We are the Dead. Short days ago
We lived, felt dawn, saw sunset glow,
Loved and were loved, and now we lie
In Flanders fields.

Take up our quarrel with the foe:
To you from failing hands we throw
The torch; be yours to hold it high.
If ye break faith with us who die
We shall not sleep, though poppies grow
In Flanders fields.

John McCrae

The Soldier

If I should die, think only this of me:
That there's some corner of a foreign field
That is for ever England. There shall be
In that rich earth a richer dust concealed;
A dust whom England bore, shaped, made aware,
Gave, once, her flowers to love, her ways to roam,
A body of England's, breathing English air,
Washed by the rivers, blest by suns of home.

And think, this heart, all evil shed away,
A pulse in the eternal mind, no less
Gives somewhere back the thoughts by England given;
Her sights and sounds; dreams happy as her day;
And laughter, learnt of friends; and gentleness,
In hearts at peace, under an English heaven.

Rupert Brooke

Dulce et Decorum Est

Bent double, like old beggars under sacks,
Knock-kneed, coughing like hags, we cursed through
    sludge,
Till on the haunting flares we turned our backs,
And towards our distant rest began to trudge.
Men marched asleep. Many had lost their boots,
But limped on, blood-shod. All went lame; all blind;
Drunk with fatigue; deaf even to the hoots
Of gas-shells dropping softly behind.

Gas! GAS! Quick, boys!—An ecstasy of fumbling
Fitting the clumsy helmets just in time;
But someone still was yelling out and stumbling
And floundering like a man in fire or lime.—
Dim, through the misty panes and thick green light
As under a green sea, I saw him drowning.

In all my dreams, before my helpless sight,
He plunges at me, guttering, choking, drowning.

If in some smothering dreams you too could pace
Behind the wagon that we flung him in,
And watch the white eyes writhing in his face,
His hanging face, like a devil's sick of sin;
If you could hear, at every jolt, the blood
Come gargling from the froth-corrupted lungs,
Obscene as cancer, bitter as the cud
Of vile, incurable sores on innocent tongues,—
My friend, you would not tell with such high zest
To children ardent for some desperate glory,
The old Lie: *Dulce et decorum est*
Pro patria mori.

Wilfred Owen

Where the River Meets the Sea

Where the river meets the sea
Where my Lord comforts me
And our troubles let us be
Where the river meets the sea

Where the river meets the land
Where the weak begin to stand
And the lost will understand
Where the river meets the land

Where the sea meets the sky
Where the wounded will fly
And the prayers come down from on high
I know I'll be standing by

Where the river meets the sea
When it sounds like a symphony
Then the blind finally see
Where the river meets the sea

Where the river is at its end
And it carries you like a friend
And the broken will begin to mend
They shall rise again

Where the river meets the sea
Where my Lord comforts me
And I know someday I'll be
Where the river meets the sea

Where love will set us free
Where the river meets the sea

Michael McDermott

It's Hard to Be Humble
(When You Look as Good as Me)

Have you got that sinking feeling
When your shoes are set for leaving
Don't you turn around
Just grin and stand your ground

Feeling tongue-tied and twisted
When this cruel world takes the biscuit?
You are what you are
You are a superstar

Why worry about it anyway
Give a wink, and smile and say . . .

It's hard to be humble
When you look as good as me
Absolutely unstoppable
The universe agrees
Take a look in the mirror
Love what you see
And say 'It's hard to be humble
When you look as good as me'

You're a walking work of art
The sum of many parts
Walk in, own the room
Walk in – boom boom boom

If your troubles come to call
Send you climbing up the wall
Don't worry any more
Show them all the door

That's how you work it out
Turn your whisper to a shout

It's hard to be humble
When you look as good as me
Absolutely unstoppable
The universe agrees
Take a look in the mirror
Love what you see
And say 'It's hard to be humble
When you look as good as me'

Ian W. Brown, Simon Johnson and Henry Priestman

A Smile

Smiling is infectious,
you catch it like the flu.
When someone smiled at me today
I started smiling too.

I passed around the corner
and someone saw my grin.
When he smiled, I realized
I'd passed it on to him.

I thought about my smile and then
I realized its worth.
A single smile like mine could travel
right around the earth.

If you feel a smile begin
don't leave it undetected.
Let's start an epidemic quick
and get the world infected.

Jez Alborough

We Just a Come

We Just a Come
Yes we just a come
Like the rivers, trees and just like the sun.

Each and every morning the sun rises at dawn
And each and every day another baby is born.
Look at the sea how it keeps on turning
Just like the sea you got to keep on learning.
Step by step the tree of life you should be climbing
Let your light shine bright never let it go dim
Though the river is deep don't be afraid to swim.

We Just a Come
Yes we just a come
Like the rivers, trees and just like the sun.

It takes many rivers to form the ocean
All types of people to build a nation.
It takes many branches to make one tree
It takes a mother and a father to raise a family.
Both need foundation and roots are the keys
Without roots you'll be swept away by the sea.

We Just a Come
Yes we just a come
Like the rivers, trees and just like the sun.

Unstoppable, incredible we're still moving on
Against all odds maybe a billion to one.
Driven by the energy we get from the sun
From the tree of life we took the wood to make a drum.
Winter turns to spring and seconds embrace the hours
Now you can't force the bud into a flower
And if the water doesn't run it must turn sour.

We Just a Come
Yes we just a come
Like the rivers, trees and just like the sun.

The sun rises and the sun must fall
Now this is a message, a message to all.
Notice how the tree stands proud and tall
Try to know yourself before your back's against the wall.
Yes we've come a long way, but the road is still long
As we rise to the challenge we will all sing this song.

We Just a Come
Yes we just a come
Like the rivers, trees and just like the sun.

Adisa

The Affirmation

These are the days
The days we won't forget
As time comes to pass
We'll be standing en masse
And we haven't started counting yet

These are the hours
The hours we won't regret
While we wait at the gates
Of the good and the great
Just like the day that we first met

These are the friends
The friends that hold no threat
They are learned and kind
With a wide open mind
About as close as you can get

These are the songs
The songs that tie the lines
While we're out on the floor
There's a promise of more
And we haven't started dancing yet

These are the debts
The debts that we won't collect
These are the friends
The friends that we don't neglect
This is the knowing

These are the debts
The debts that we don't collect
These are the friends
The friends that we won't neglect
This is the knowing

Miles Hunt

Brian Moses

'I Remember, I Remember' by Thomas Hood on page 53

In this poem, the poet is thinking back to his childhood days, and of the things that brought him pleasure – the morning sun peeping though his window, the robin's nest among the lilacs, playing on a swing, the high dark fir trees seeming as if they almost touched the sky.

We also understand from this poem that, although the poet's present life is less carefree and that his spirit is 'so heavy now', he still finds comfort in his memories.

The poem sings to me as I read it and I can hear a background of tinkling bells, a xylophone, shakers and a drumbeat on each rhyming word. Try it, don't be afraid to experiment with sounds that can help to heighten the atmosphere of the piece.

We all have a treasure chest of memories that we keep in our heads and I certainly enjoy looking back at mine. Children too will be storing up their own memories, and these can be used to promote their own writing.

Ask children to think of a memory, maybe a place – perhaps the best place ever visited – or a creature they once knew, maybe a dog or a cat that their grandparents had which they loved to play with when they visited. Or think of a memory of a person – a friend who has moved away, someone who became a holiday friend but hasn't been seen since. Or perhaps an event, a really special wedding day, a party or a trip to Alton Towers.

Get children to mind-map their memories so that

before they start writing they have some ideas ready. My mind map of Paris would be: smell of baguettes, early morning mist on the Seine, red and white lights winking from the Eiffel Tower at night, chatter in cafes, cold gloomy catacombs, etc.

Remind children to focus on the magic of their memories and not the mundane.

Once they have their ideas, remind them that they shouldn't worry about making the poem rhyme, rather concentrate on a rhythm though repetition of one or two words maximum.

Try starting every other line with 'I remember' (not every line, that would be too repetitive) or use 'memories' as a rhythm word in the same way:

> Memories of the time we saw the sign
> leading us to a week of fun, sand, sun
> and boogie boarding on the waves.
>
> Memories of exploring secret rock pools,
> hiding from prying eyes,
> swimming in fresh clear water lagoons,
> pulling my sister along behind me.
>
> Memories . . .

David Harmer

'The Door' by Miroslav Holub on page 132

I've always loved this poem. It is very simple and straightforward in form as it falls down the page with the key word 'Go' capitalized, followed by 'and open the door.' It is an active poem; it tells the reader to do something, to open a door and see what they find. Also it helps children realize that poetry doesn't always rhyme and to attempt that difficult skill can limit them. This is a poem of no limits at all. So many things can lie the other side of a door. Doors, like keys, are potent symbols of 'what if?' because they conjure up a diverse range of possibilities for the imagination to explore.

One way of reading/performing the poem is to divide the sections between different groups of pupils but have them all say 'Go and open the door'. Or have one group just saying that and the lines are then split between other groups. This combination of group voices and whole-class voices can be added to by giving certain children a solo line. Another possibility is to have some children whisper 'Go and open the door' as a repeated, underlying pattern, as others speak lines from the poem over the top. Some lines suggest certain vocal effects, like the 'darkness ticking', where the key word, ticking, can be repeated/faded away by some voices in the group. The same goes for the 'hollow wind' or the ending, where some or all the voices could make a sound effect of whistling, whooshing air.

A lot of the lines can start a child's own writing. They can write a poem about the face they see, closely describing its features. Then they can invent what it says and how it speaks. Does it whisper? Does it shout? Is it scary? Whose face is it? A giant? A friend? A gorgon? Does it fill the whole door or is it in the distance? Is the 'eye' behind the door part of that face? Lots of other lines can be a launching pad for the children. They can write poems about exploring the 'ticking darkness' and the 'hollow wind' that blows there. Are they in a forest at night, full of monsters and strange noises? Is it a castle, a beach, their home, a station, a strange country, an island, another planet, a ruined mansion? Are they alone or with others? Have they travelled in time? Are they somewhere they know but long after their lifetime?

Like the doors they open into their imaginations, the possibilities are endless.

Jan Dean

'The Sound Collector' by Roger McGough on page 85

This is a very clever list poem wrapped up in the idea of stolen sound – itself a playful explanation for silence. Because it's about sound the poem is packed with onomatopoeia, so it's brilliant out loud. Try exaggerating the 'sound' words in performance – groups could do this. Or give each child one sound word each that they repeat quietly until the sound collector (that's you reading the poem out loud) takes their word and the room slowly becomes silent.

- You could adapt this idea for the other senses and write about 'The Colour Thief', 'The Scent Stealer' or 'The Taker of Textures'.
- Or you could 'explode' an image by choosing one phrase and developing it, e.g. Take 'the whistling of the kettle' and turn it round to 'the kettle whistled like . . . like what? What whistles? A train/a bird/the wind.
- Play with the ideas. The kettle whistled like a hot and angry bird/like a white bird in the wild wind. Write out the images on a large piece of paper, cut them up and shuffle them around. See what you can come up with. Follow the idea wherever it leads. Hear the wild white whistle of the wind bird/watch the wind bird fly/ feel the steamy wingbeats of the wind bird/in the wild white sky . . .
- Spend some time in silence with your eyes closed, collecting sounds. Go for a silent walk in the

playground/nature area with a notepad – make marks on the paper 'drawing' the sounds you hear. Use your sound collection/marks to write your own list poem which will be a picture in sound of the place where you heard them.

- Make a sound map of your classroom/any other room. Use colours and symbols for the different noises. Write about the map you've made. Think how your symbols and colours might become words, e.g. the sellotape machine gives a squeak like a yellow rubber band screaming.
- Write a poem giving directions not by landmarks, but by 'soundmarks', e.g. a walk through a wood might begin 'walk through the song of small brown birds/ turn left at the snapping of twigs/be careful not to trip over the rustling of squirrels, etc.

Paul Cookson

'Daddy Fell into the Pond' by Alfred Noyes on page 48

This was the first poem I remember from my primary-school days. I don't think a teacher read it to us, I think I borrowed a book from our after-school library every Monday.

Of course, it's the title that's memorable and gives the poem its comedy. In my own mind I'd pictured Daddy in the pond because he was trying to rescue a cat from a tree. When I rediscovered the poem later in life there were no references to cats, ladders or trees. This had all been part of the illustration and as such had woven itself into the poem and my subsequent memory of the poem.

That's what I love – the cartoon and comic aspect of the poem. The title says it all, draws us in and gives us that cartoon image. And that is a great starting point.

The rest of the poem does what it needs to do, the rhymes are fine and there's not much of a story (apart from the fact that the family must have been quite well off to have had a 'gardener') – but it's the joy of the repeated line . . .

Daddy fell into the pond!

I have a poem called 'When the Wasp Flew Up My Brother's Shorts', and I always say that once you've heard the title I almost don't need to do the poem as your imagination has already done the rest.

So – let's have that as a starting point. A cartoon title where you get an immediate picture and that leads you into the poem and the subsequent ideas.

Either...

Use the fact that Daddy has fallen into the pond as a starting point...

How did he fall into the pond?

What was he doing?

Was he playing a game?

Was it a trick played on him by his children?

Was he in his best clothes?

Think of the strangest reasons he could have ended up in the pond.

All these are part of the whole story – now, fill in the gaps – what, when, how, why, who, etc.

You could still use *Daddy fell into the pond* as a repeated line. I wouldn't worry too much about making the poem rhyme – more that every four lines or so you repeat the funny line. Get the class to join in with it.

OR...

Think of your own comic title:

    The day that Dad split his trousers
    When Mum spilt ice cream down her dress
    Sister's in the fish tank
    Baby Brother is stuck in the cupboard
    The day our teacher fell in the bin
    When Grandad's false teeth shot out

Once you start I'm sure the class will come up with lots of possibilities.

Again, work backwards from the punchline – fill in the story, build it up, bit by bit.

Exaggerate, make it larger than life, make it as cartoony as possible.

Every so often – maybe every four lines – repeat the line.

Have fun!

Coral Rumble

'Stopping by Woods on a Snowy Evening' by Robert Frost on page 12

I love this poem for many reasons. It has a very simple 'surface meaning', but it also holds other, special meanings for readers. Poems can often be interpreted in different ways, that's part of the intrigue of them! The poem tells the story of someone stopping to take in a beautiful scene before hurrying on to resume his everyday life of commitments. Personally, I love the peace of the poem, as it whispers in the silence. Listen to all those 's' sounds, telling us to shush!

DISCUSSION TIPS
Sound is very important in most poems, and this one uses 'sound effects' with mastery. I refer to rhyme as 'sound echoes', and sometimes those echoes are strong and obvious, sometimes they are subtler. After discussing the story of the poem, you could discuss a number of sonic qualities in this poem with your class:

1. There is a very firm rhyme scheme – aaba, bbcb, ccdc, dddd. The first, second and fourth lines rhyme, and the third line sets up the rhyme sound for the next stanza, apart from in stanza four, where the same end of line rhyme comes throughout.

Ask your children to work out the rhyme scheme used, with the letter code above. Remind them that poetry has a lot to do with patterns. In this poem we have patterns of rhyme, rhythm and stanza length. Children often enjoy the discovery of this.

2. There is much internal rhyme in the poem. You'll find consonance and assonance alongside perfect rhyme. Ask your children about the effect of all the 's' sounds. Ask them whether it helps to create silence or stillness.

3. Discuss the effect of the repetition of a line at the end. It could indicate that other concerns are being repeated in his mind, like a nagging thought. It could indicate a return to reality, or be an encouragement to himself to get moving. THERE IS NO RIGHT ANSWER!

PERFORMANCE TIP
In performance, the sounds of the poem will come through. Children should not be asked to emphasize sounds too much; Robert Frost has done all the hard work for us! Obviously the poem should be delivered in a quiet manner. Effective and clear diction can make up for any volume lost. You could direct a child to read it like they're telling a secret.

USE IN CLASS
There are many ways this poem can be used in class.

I would definitely use it as a springboard for all sorts of discussion:

Starting Points
1. Ask your children to retell stories from their own lives, when one small moment seemed important.

2. Ask your children to list some loud/hard words (truck, bang, etc.) or quiet/gentle words (feather, trickle, etc.). Then ask them to write a poem where they use loud or quiet words as 'sound effects'.

3. Ask your children to write a poem about the 'small moment' they discussed in point 1.

Index of First Lines

Index of Poets

Acknowledgements

The compiler and publisher would like to thank the following for permission to use copyright material:

Adisa, 'Future Masterpiece' and 'We Just a Come' by permission of the author; **Agard, John,** 'Secret' by permission of Caroline Sheldon Literary Agency on behalf of the author; **Ahlberg, Allan,** 'Please Mrs Butler' from *Collected Poems*, Penguin Books Ltd 2008; **Alborough, Jez,** 'A Smile' by permission of the author; **Andrew, Moira,** 'My Gran' from *Fun with Poems* (Brilliant Publications) by permission of the author; **Auden, W. H.,** 'The Night Mail' by permission of Curtis Brown Ltd on behalf of the author; **Ayres, Pam,** 'Oh, I Wish I'd Looked After Me Teeth' from *The Works* by Pam Ayres, published by BBC Books © Pam Ayres, 1992, 2008. Reproduced by permission of Sheil Land Associates Ltd; **Berry, James,** 'People Equal' by permission of the author; **Bloom, Valerie,** 'The River' by permission of the author; **Bragg, Billy,** 'Song of the Iceberg' Words and Music by Billy Bragg © 2012 and 'Tank Park Salute' Words and Music by Billy Bragg © 1991, both reproduced by permission of Sony/ATV Music Publishing (UK) Limited, London W1F 9LD; **Breis,** 'Think Big' by permission of the author; **Brown, Ian W.,** 'It's Hard to Be Humble (When You Look as Good as Me)' by permission of the author; **Brownlee, Liz,** 'Slithering Silver' by permission of the author; **Calder, Dave,** 'Changed' from *Dolphins Leap Lampposts* (Macmillan, 2002) by permission of the author; **Carter, James,** 'Take a Poem' from *Time-Travelling Underpants* by James Carter (Macmillan, 2007) by permission of the author; **Causley, Charles,** 'Timothy Winters' from *I Had a Little Cat – Collected Poems For Children* by permission of David Higham Associates Ltd on behalf of the author; **Coelho, Joseph,** 'Conquer' from *Werewolf Club Rules*, Frances Lincoln Children's Books 2014; **Cookson, Paul,** 'Let No One Steal Your Dreams', 'This Is Our School', 'We Are the Writers' and 'May You Always' all by permission of the author; **Cooper**

Clarke, John, 'Nation's Ode to the Coast' by Dr John Cooper Clarke was commissioned by the National Trust to celebrate the Year of the Coast in 2015 and inspired by over 11,000 coastal thoughts, memories and images contributed by the British public; **Corbett, Pie,** 'Evidence of a Dragon' and 'The Things Around You' from *Evidence of Dragons* by Pie Corbett (Macmillan Children's Books, 2011) © Pie Corbett; **Cullimore, Stan,** 'If I Could Choose' by permission of the author; **Dean, Jan,** 'Angels' by permission of the author; **Denton, Graham,** 'I Think My Teacher's Wonderful' from *My Rhino Plays the Xylophone: Poems to Make You Giggle* by Graham Denton (A&C Black, 2014) by permission of the author; **Dixon, Peter,** 'Lone Mission' by permission of the author; **Donaldson, Julia,** 'Class Photograph' and 'The Mouse and the Lion', from *Crazy Mayonnaisy Mum*, Macmillan Children's Books (2004), reproduced by kind permission of Julia Donaldson c/o Caroline Sheldon Literary Agency; **Duffy, Carol Ann,** 'Teacher' from *The Good Child's Guide to Rock 'n' Roll* (Faber, 2003) by permission of Rogers, Coleridge and White on behalf of the author; **Edgar, Marriott,** 'The Lion and Albert' words and music by George Marriott Edgar (1933), reproduced with permission of EMI music Publishing Limited; **Edwards, Richard,** 'Some Favourite Words' by permission of the author; **Farjeon, Eleanor,** 'A Morning Song' from 'Blackbird Has Spoken' by permission of David Higham Associates Ltd on behalf of the author; **Foster, John,** 'Four O'Clock Friday' copyright © John Foster 1991 from *Four O'Clock Friday* (Oxford University Press) by permission of the author; **Frost, Robert,** 'Stopping by Woods on a Snowy Evening' from *The Poetry of Robert Frost* edited by Edward Connery Latham, reprinted by permission of The Random House Group ltd; **Gittins, Chrissie,** 'What Will I Put in my Suitcase When I Go to Visit the Stars?' from *The Caterpillar – Magazine of Stories, Poems and Art for Kids,* Issue 6 (Autumn 2014) by permission of the author; **Glynn, Martin,** 'Wurd Up' by permission of the author; **Goodfellow, Matt,** 'With the Waterfalls' and 'Thought Cloud' by permission of the author; **Harding, Mike,** 'Christmas Market'

by permission of the author; **Harmer, David,** 'Mister Moore' from *The Works* (Macmillan Children's Books, edited by Paul Cookson, 1991) and 'Our Tree' from *Earthways Earthwise* (Oxford University Press, edited by Judith Nicholls, 1993) by permission of the author; **Hegley, John,** 'What a Poem's Not' from *My Dog Is a Carrot* published by Walker Books by permission of United Agents; **Henderson, Stewart,** 'My Mother Smells . . .' from *Poetry Emotion* by Stewart Henderson © (Barnabus in Schools, 2012) by permission of the author; **Holub, Miroslav,** 'The Door' by permission of Bloodaxe Books; **Hunt, Miles,** 'The Affirmation' by permission of Spirit Music and Media Ltd on behalf of the author; **Joseph, Jenny,** 'The Magic of the Brain' by permission of the author; **Kay, Jackie,** 'Word of a Lie' from *The Frog Who Dreamt She Was An Opera Singer* by permission of Bloomsbury Publishing PLC; **Knight, Stephen,** 'The Long Grass' from *Sardines and Other Poems* by Stephen Knight (Young Picador, 2004) by permission of the author; **McDermott, Michael,** 'Where the River Meets the Sea' by permission of the author; **McGough, Roger,** 'Everything Touches' from *Lucky* Frances Lincoln Children's Books and 'The Sound Collector' from *Pillow Talk* (1990) Puffin Books reprinted by permission of Peters Fraser & Dunlop on behalf of the author; **McMillan, Ian,** 'Adult Fiction' by permission of the author; **Mitton, Tony,** 'Forbidden Poem' by permission of David Higham Associates Ltd on behalf of the author; **Moses, Brian,** 'A Feather from an Angel' and 'Walking with My Iguana' from *The Very Best of Brian Moses* (Macmillan Children's Books, 2016) © Brian Moses; **Nichols, Grace,** 'Give Yourself a Hug' from *Give Yourself A Hug*, A&C Black. By permission of Grace Nichols c/o Curtis Brown Limited; **Noyes, Alfred,** 'Daddy Fell into the Pond' by permission of The Society of Authors as the Literary Representative of Alfred Noyes; **Ousbey, Jack,** 'Gran Can You Rap?' by permission of the author; **Owen, Gareth,** 'Den to Let' by permission of the author; **Patten, Brian,** 'Geography Lesson' and 'Reading the Classics' © Brian Patten c/o Rogers, Coleridge and White, 20 Powis Mews, London

W11 1JN; **Priestman, Henry,** 'It's Hard to Be Humble (When You Look as Good as Me)' by permission of the author; **Rice, John,** 'Do You Know My Teacher?' copyright © John Rice 2005, from *The Secret Lives of Teachers* (edited by Brian Moses, Macmillan Children's Books) by permission of the author; **Rooney, Rachel,** 'A Girl' by permission of the author; **Rumble, Coral,** 'Nativity in 20 Seconds' from *Breaking The Rules* by Coral Rumble (Lion Children's, 2004) by permission of the author; **Scannell, Vernon,** 'The Apple Raid' by permission of The Estate of Vernon Scannell; **Sissay, Lemn,** 'Let There Be Peace' by permission of the author; **Stephenson, Martin,** 'Home' written by Martin G. Stephenson for his mother Frances Anne Stephenson, sadly departed through cancer in 2003; **Stevens, Roger,** 'List of Lists' from *The Monster That Ate the Universe* (Macmillan Children's Books, 2004) by permission by the author; **Stonier, Nigel,** 'I Hope I Always' by permission of the author; **Toczek, Nick,** 'The Dragon Who Ate Our School' from *Dragons Are Back!* (Caboodle Books, 2016) and *Dragons!* (Macmillan Children's Books, 2005) both of which were collections of Nick Toczek's dragon poems, by permission of the author; **Turner, Steve,** 'I Like Words' from *The Day I Fell Down the Toilet* (Oxford; Lion, 1996) by permission of the author; **Warren, Celia,** 'I Do as Simon Says' © Celia Warren, from *Taking My Human for a Walk* (edited by Roger Stevens, Macmillan 2003) by permission of the author; **Webster, Clive,** 'The Magic of the Mind' by permission of the author; **West, Colin,** 'My Colours' © Colin West. Reprinted with permission; **Wright, Kit,** 'The Magic Box' by permission of the author; **Young, Bernard,** 'Best Friends' by permission of the author; **Zephaniah, Benjamin,** 'Body Talk' from *Talking Turkeys* by permission of Penguin Publishers Ltd.

Every effort has been made to trace the copyright holders, but if any have been inadvertently overlooked the publisher will be pleased to make the necessary arrangement at the first opportunity.